"What are we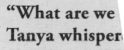
Tanya whisper

"Do about what?"

She stood before him—not close enough that they touched but close enough that he could smell her. Feel her breath against his skin. He clenched his teeth.

"You want me, don't you?"

"We had an agreement. I pay your expenses on the road in exchange for your help with Alex. This wasn't part of the deal."

She moved her fingers south, grazing the waistband of his boxers. "What if we redefine the boundaries?"

He swallowed hard. Vic wasn't sure how long he could let her touch him and not reciprocate.

"This isn't part of the deal." She nuzzled his ear. "It's just..." She nipped his neck. "It's whatever we want it to be."

Vic spun, pressing Tanya against the door. Tanya's tongue slipped inside his mouth and he forgot all the reasons this was wrong.

Dear Reader,

I've been waiting to tell Victor Vicario's story for a long time, and I hope you enjoy the final installment of the Cowboys of the Rio Grande series. All of the heroes in this series have had to overcome tough childhoods, but Victor's journey was perhaps the most difficult.

I love including children in my books, because little ones have a way of teaching adults life lessons that might otherwise pass us over. When Vic is called home to take responsibility for a nephew he'd never met before, he has no intention of caring for the boy long-term. And no one is more surprised than Vic when a little boy who's afraid to talk teaches him that letting go of the past is the only way forward.

I hope you enjoy Victor's story, and if you missed the previous books in this series, *A Cowboy's Redemption* (June 2015) and *The Surgeon's Christmas Baby* (November 2015), you can find more information about these stories and other books I've written at marinthomas.com.

Happy reading,

Marin Thomas

A COWBOY'S CLAIM

MARIN THOMAS

HARLEQUIN® AMERICAN ROMANCE®

Recycling programs
for this product may
not exist in your area.

ISBN-13: 978-0-373-75615-5

A Cowboy's Claim

Copyright © 2016 by Brenda Smith-Beagley

Printed in U.S.A.

Marin Thomas grew up in the Midwest, then attended college at the U of A in Tucson, Arizona, where she earned a BA in radio-TV and played basketball for the Lady Wildcats. Following graduation, she married her college sweetheart in the historic Little Chapel of the West in Las Vegas, Nevada. Recent empty nesters, Marin and her husband now live in Texas, where cattle is king, cowboys are plentiful and pickups rule the road. Visit her on the web at marinthomas.com.

Books by Marin Thomas

Harlequin American Romance

The Cash Brothers

The Cowboy Next Door
Twins Under the Christmas Tree
Her Secret Cowboy
The Cowboy's Destiny
True Blue Cowboy
A Cowboy of Her Own

Rodeo Rebels

Rodeo Daddy
The Bull Rider's Secret
A Rodeo Man's Promise
Arizona Cowboy
A Cowboy's Duty
No Ordinary Cowboy

Cowboys of the Rio Grande

A Cowboy's Redemption
The Surgeon's Christmas Baby

Visit the Author Profile page
at Harlequin.com for more titles.

To my furry pals Bandit and Rascal,
who have kept watch over me and
my writing for the past fourteen years.
You were snoozing at my feet when
I sold my first book and you're
snoozing now as I write this.
Thank you for blessing our family with
your devotion, cuteness and love.

Prologue

The wipers were no match for the torrential downpour pummeling the windshield. Victor Vicario strained to see the road ten feet in front of his pickup. After competing in the Houston Livestock Show and Rodeo, he was tired, but it was a good tired. Pocketing a check for twenty-five thousand dollars had a way of easing his aches and pain.

He glanced at the boot-shaped trophy resting on the passenger seat. He'd find a UPS store tomorrow and mail the award to his former high school teacher Maria Alvarez Fitzgerald, who'd helped him earn his GED. After he'd announced his intention to join the rodeo circuit, she'd managed to keep a straight face when she volunteered to safeguard his trophies. No one, including himself, had believed he'd ever succeed in the sport. But over a decade later he was still chasing the one win that had eluded him.

The first few years on the circuit had been the worst—trying to do it all on his own. When he'd finally admitted he needed help, former world-champion saddle bronc rider Riley Fitzgerald took him under his wing and had taught him how to keep his backside in the saddle and win. Then Vic had gone out on his own and made a name for himself. The past five years he'd won or placed in the top three of most major rodeos—except the National Finals Rodeo in Las Vegas.

He refused to hang up his spurs until he won a national title.

This year would end differently—he felt it in his gut. He was thirty-one—young in mind, old in body. Broken bones, sprained wrists and horse kicks had taken a toll on him, but he was starting out a new season in the best shape he'd ever been. A lot of months and a lot of rides stood between Vic and the NFR in December. All it took was one nasty fall to wipe out a life's worth of hard work, but he'd left Houston without a scratch and that was a good sign.

A vehicle with its flashers on came into view. He eased off the accelerator, thinking he should have sat out the bad weather in a motel room. But he wanted to make it to Beaumont tonight and then rest for a few days before he rode in the South Texas State Fair. He checked his side mirror before changing lanes.

The pickup and horse trailer sat on the shoulder—maybe a competitor from the rodeo. As he drove past he spotted the Red Rock Horse Farm logo on the pickup door. Tanya McGee—the feisty barrel racer who could hardly control her horse. She hadn't competed in the Houston rodeo, but he'd seen her in the stands, watching her competition. Vic had never spoken to Tanya in person, but he'd noticed her auburn hair and eyes bluer than the New Mexico sky.

Since he didn't socialize with the cowboys on the circuit, the only thing he knew about the pretty cowgirl was what he'd heard others say near the chutes. Tanya had been married to Vic's competitor Beau Billings. Everyone knew Beau Billings rode more than broncs when he showed up at rodeos. Vic assumed Tanya had been attracted to Billings's movie-star looks, but it wasn't long after they'd married that the jerk began two-timing her. Billings was a womanizer in the worst way, and Tanya had done herself a favor when she kicked the cheater to the curb.

Vic pulled onto the shoulder in front of Tanya's truck and turned on his flashers. He'd see if she was waiting out the storm or if she'd run into mechanical problems. He reached for his old Stetson and put it on to protect him from the rain, then stepped from his pickup. Tanya flipped on her brights and almost blinded him. He stopped at the driver's-side window and she lowered it a couple of inches.

"Everything okay?" he shouted. When she didn't answer, he said, "It's Vic Vicario. You need help?" He wasn't vain, but he had enough wins on his résumé that most rodeo athletes knew him by name.

The window lowered farther, the blowing rain pelting Tanya in the face. "The trailer has a flat tire."

The nearest exit was five miles up the highway—a drive that far on a flat tire with an undisciplined horse inside the trailer was a disaster waiting to happen. Tanya's horse, an American paint gelding, was famous on the circuit and not in a good way. "I can change the flat, but you'll have to take Slingshot out of the trailer. Can you keep him under control in this weather?"

Her chin jutted—as if he'd offended her—and then her shoulders slumped. "I don't know."

At least she was honest. The horse was faster than the wind but unpredictable. Slingshot had thrown Tanya the few times he saw the pair compete. Why she stuck with the renegade was anybody's guess. "Will you be able to change the flat, if I hold on to Slingshot?"

"Maybe."

"You can't sit on the side of the road," he said. "It's too dangerous for you and the horse."

She put on a baseball cap sporting a Denver Broncos logo, then got out of the pickup. She was short—maybe five-six if that. Vic topped out at six feet in his boots and he towered over her small, wiry frame.

"I'll fetch my toolbox," he said. "Wait until I get back before you unload him." He returned to his pickup, grabbed the tire jack and a wrench and set the tools on the ground next to the flat.

"Watch out," Tanya said. She unlatched the trailer door and stepped inside. Vic heard her speak to Slingshot as she backed him down the ramp. He stood ready to help, but she coaxed him to follow her into the gully along the highway without incident. "Okay, we're good!"

As soon as she spoke, thunder rumbled overhead and the horse reared.

"You got him?"

Vic started down the incline but stopped when she held up a hand. "I'm not helpless."

Tanya McGee was the furthest thing from helpless Vic had ever encountered. He changed the flat tire, moving as fast as possible. He'd just tightened the last lug nut when lightning sizzled across the sky. Tanya held on to the reins, but lost her footing on the wet ground and slid under the gelding. Vic scrambled down the embankment, falling on his butt once before reaching the pair. He took the reins with one hand and wrapped an arm around Tanya's waist with the other, then hauled her out from beneath the belly of the beast.

The horse reared a second time. "Whoa, boy." Vic wished he'd thought to put on his riding glove. The rope burned his hands as Slingshot pulled hard to get free. Tanya talked nonsense to the animal until he quit stomping his hooves against the ground.

Tanya and her beloved horse shared a bond, but it baffled him that she couldn't control the animal in the arena. "Ready?" he asked, taking hold of the noseband while she grasped the reins. They escorted Slingshot back to the trailer, where he was more than happy to load and get out of the storm.

Tanya locked the door. "Thank goodness he didn't bolt." She'd lost her baseball cap, and the rain had plastered her hair to her face and her clothes to her body, leaving little to the imagination. She shoved the hair out of her eyes and caught him staring at her bosom. He considered apologizing, but what for? He didn't care what Tanya McGee thought of him. Her gaze moved to the scar on his face—if he was scary-looking in the daylight, he must be terrifying in the dark.

"Get off the road as soon as possible," he said. "The spare tire is in bad shape."

"I'll take the next exit." When he made a move to step past her, she grasped his shirtsleeve. "Thank you, Victor."

"Drive safe." He waited in his pickup until Tanya pulled out in front of him and then he followed at a distance. She drove below the speed limit, so he didn't bother turning off his flashers. When she took the exit to the Buc-ee's Travel Center, he trailed her into the parking lot but remained in his pickup while she searched for a parking spot. She disappeared inside and he continued to wait—why, he didn't know.

A few minutes later Tanya stepped outside, holding two coffees. She signaled him to come in, but he didn't care to stand in front of her beneath the harsh fluorescent lights and watch her try not to stare at his scar.

He honked and then hit the gas and sped away.

As he merged onto the highway, he rubbed the thick knot of skin along the side of his face. The accident had happened eighteen years ago.

Accident. His wound hadn't been an accident, but calling it anything else was too painful.

Chapter One

"Ladies and gentlemen, welcome to Stampede Park in beautiful sunny Cody, Wyoming! We're expecting record-breaking temperatures this first week of July, so be sure you're drinking plenty of water. If you're looking for a seat in the shade, we still have a few available under the Buzzard Roost."

The grandstand took up one side, the rough stock and cowboys the other. The scent of greasy burgers, popcorn, cigarettes and sweaty bodies permeated the air until you got close to the chutes. Then the heavy stink of nervous bucking stock and the stuff that comes out of their back ends stole your breath—unless you were immune to it as Vic was.

Garth Brooks's song "Rodeo" blasted through the loudspeakers for a few seconds. Then the announcer continued his spiel. "It's been a wild start to Cowboy Christmas here in the cowboy state. For those of you who aren't familiar with the term Cowboy Christmas…"

Vic paced behind the chute, where Snake Oil Willie waited patiently for him. Why did every damned rodeo announcer feel compelled to explain Cowboy

Christmas to the fans? People wanted to see cowboys go head-to-head with the bucking stock—they didn't care that this was the time of year cowboys ramped up their earnings to help them qualify for the National Finals Rodeo in December. Only the top fifteen cowboys made it to Vegas, and Vic intended to be one of them.

He was bone tired after his midnight ride in the Greeley Independence Stampede in Colorado, four hundred fifty miles away. He'd driven all night to get to Cody, and the five days before that he'd been in Pecos, Texas. As soon as he competed today, he was back in his truck heading to Red Lodge, Montana, sixty miles up the interstate where he was due to ride at three. Then he had to make it to the Round Top Rodeo in Livingston, one hundred twenty-three miles farther down the road, for his last go-round of the day. He'd taken first place in Greeley, and if he finished in the top three in his last two rodeos of the day, he could earn close to five thousand dollars.

"We're fortunate to have a superstar among our competitors today. Victor Vicario is currently ranked twelve in the PRCA standings. He started off the year on a high note, taking first place at the Houston Livestock Show and Rodeo back in March."

The din increased and Vic slipped farther into the shadows of the cowboy ready area. He didn't care for all the attention that came with winning. As soon as he claimed a national title, he intended to disappear from the rodeo scene. If he never rode another bronc the rest of his life, that would be fine with him.

"Last year Vicario ended his season in fourth place

at the NFR in Vegas and you can bet he's aiming to return for another chance to win the title."

Once the crowd quieted, the announcer mentioned other cowboys competing today. Vic blocked out the noise and drew his thoughts inward as he prepared for his ride. He recalled his best ride, which happened to be last year in Vegas. He imagined every detail right down to the smells of the bucking chute, the heat coming off Sun River Bay's back and the sound of the gelding's snorts. Once Vic completed the ride in his head, he opened his eyes.

He was first out of the gate in his event—fine by him. He intended to set the bar high and intimidate his competition. He could thank the barrio in Albuquerque for his cutthroat attitude. Vic hadn't grown up on a farm or a ranch like most rodeo cowboys. He hadn't shown a cow or a pig in the local 4-H fair. Instead, he'd spent his free time tagging public property, stealing sodas and candy from convenience stores, skipping school and pledging gangs.

"Vicario will be coming out of chute two on Snake Oil Willie. This bronc can two-step like nobody's business."

When the rodeo helper signaled him, Vic stepped into the open. No one wished him good luck on his walk to the chute. He was good at busting broncs, but the scar on his face and his brooding personality kept anyone from trying to be his friend. Sometimes the loneliness got to him, but it was a fitting penance considering his high school pal Cruz Rivera had spent twelve years behind bars because of Vic.

He climbed the rails and straddled the bronc. Snake Oil Willie's muscles bunched beneath Vic's weight, but the horse behaved. Vic had never ridden the gelding in competition and had heard rumors that good ol' Willie was full of tricks once he escaped the chute.

Vic adjusted his grip on the thick rein attached to the horse's halter, took a deep breath, then nodded to the gate man and braced himself for liftoff. As soon as the chute opened, Snake Oil Willie rocketed into the air. Instinct took over and Vic placed his spurs against the points of the horse's shoulders then marked out. With his left arm high in the air, he squeezed the bronc's withers and spurred front to back, keeping his toes pointing outward. The first few bucks were smooth and controlled, but then the bronc tensed beneath him and Vic relaxed his hold on the rein, trying to avoid a spin.

Not a chance—Snake Oil Willie was too smart. The trickster spun right, forcing Vic to move with him in the saddle or get thrown off. When the bronc straightened out, Vic waited for another buck, but the horse reared and he slid backward. With a surge of strength he clung to the saddle; then the gelding's front hooves hit the dirt, jarring Vic's spine. The bronc managed to buck twice more before the buzzer sounded. Vic waited for an opening to dismount. When he saw his chance, he dove for the ground and rolled away from the clashing hooves.

The pickup men escorted Snake Oil Willie out of the arena and Vic plucked his hat from the dirt. His gaze scanned the crowd on his way back to the chutes and he caught a flash of red. Tanya McGee. What was she doing here?

Maybe she came to watch you.

No way. He hadn't run into her on the circuit since that stormy night outside Houston when he rebuffed her offer to have coffee at the truck stop. He made eye contact and nodded.

"There you have it, folks," the announcer said. "Victor Vicario scored an eighty-nine and got the best of Snake Oil Willie!"

Vic retrieved his duffel and stuffed his gear inside. He swung the bag over his shoulder and headed to the nearest concession stand to buy a corn dog for the road. He had two and a half hours before his next ride in Red Lodge.

"Victor."

Tanya. He stopped walking and waited until she caught up with him.

"Great ride."

He nodded, tongue-tied. Why did the spitfire barrel racer shove him off balance with just a smile?

"I wanted to thank you again for changing the flat on my trailer," she said. "Couldn't have been an easy feat in that downpour."

"Glad to help." He rubbed the ache in his left shoulder. He'd clipped it coming out of the chute.

She shuffled her black boots, then zeroed in on his face. Maybe it was the glare from the sun, but her eyes appeared bluer than he'd remembered.

"Did you compete today?" he asked.

She shook her head. "I'm giving Slingshot a rest, hoping it will improve his disposition."

Vic grinned before he remembered the action stretched the scar across his face, twisting the puckered flesh. "Slingshot is a handful."

"I'm well aware everyone believes my horse would be put to better use making glue."

Vic quirked an eyebrow.

"But I'm not giving up on him."

He understood how difficult it was to throw in the towel and admit defeat. He'd been hauling around twelve years of I-don't-give-up on his back. Tanya didn't appear in a hurry, but he was at a loss for something to say. He wasn't used to talking to women he respected. He only had experience with ladies after a good time and a quick goodbye.

"I came up here to look at a stud horse with my stepfather and we stopped to take in the rodeo." She waved a hand toward the parking lot. "Where are you headed next?"

"Red Lodge and then later tonight, Livingston."

She gaped at him. "You're riding in three events today?"

He opened his mouth to ask when she planned to compete again, but she cut him off.

"Damn."

"What's wrong?" he asked.

"I was hoping to avoid him today."

Vic followed her gaze—Beau Billings. "I'm hungry for a corn dog. Want to come with me?"

"Sure. Thanks." Her smile flashed brighter than the

hot sun and suddenly Vic's Wranglers felt tight in the crotch. If he survived the craziness of the first week of July, he'd think about getting laid. Right now rodeo came before pleasure.

After they joined the line at the concession stand, Tanya said, "I wish he'd quit pestering me."

"What's your ex doing to bother you?"

She wiped the perspiration off her brow, drawing Vic's attention to the smattering of freckles across her nose. She appeared younger than the twenty-six years listed in the rodeo program by her name. "He tells me every chance he gets that my horse is stupid."

Vic chuckled and then sobered when she jabbed her elbow into his ribs. "Sorry."

"It's been three years since I divorced Beau and he still acts like he has a claim on me."

He didn't know the details of her and Billings's breakup—only that she'd caught the jerk cheating. He wasn't sure if she'd walked away from barrel racing because of the divorce or the broken leg she'd suffered in a car accident a few years ago. And he sure as heck didn't know why she'd returned to the circuit on a stubborn horse like Slingshot. That Vic was interested in her situation at all surprised him even more.

"You'd think he'd have his hands full trying to please his harem of buckle bunnies that he wouldn't have time to pester me." She rolled her eyes. "The poor stupid women can't see past his handsome face and sexy voice."

That was one thing Vic didn't have to worry about—

misleading the ladies. His voice wasn't sexy and neither were his looks.

They were next in line to order—both asked for a corn dog and soda and they shared a large order of fries. Tanya insisted on paying—to thank him for his roadside assistance. They returned to the stands to eat.

She sipped her cola, then asked, "What about you, Victor? Any ex-girlfriends or wives giving you grief?"

Was Tanya making polite conversation or did she really want to know if he was involved with another woman? "No exes or girlfriends." Just him. Alone.

"So the rumors are true," she said.

"What rumors?"

"That you're a loner." She snatched the fry out of his fingers. "When Beau and I traveled the circuit together, the only competitor he ever obsessed over was you. You got under his skin."

"I barely know the guy."

"Doesn't matter. You bother Beau because he can't figure out what you're thinking."

Half the time Vic didn't *know* what he was thinking.

"You scare him and it's not because of the scar on your face." Her casual mention of his disfigurement took Vic by surprise. "Sure, the scar makes you appear intimidating and unapproachable, but there's more to it than that."

Really?

"Beau knows he doesn't have your natural ability."

Vic swallowed the last bite of his corn dog. "It's not talent, it's hard work."

"Whatever you want to call it. Beau doesn't have your smarts."

Damn, Tanya was good for his ego.

"A lot of cowboys study the way you ride, but none of them, including Beau, has ever picked up on the way you hold the buck rein." She smiled. "But I did."

Learning that his competition paid close attention to his performances was unnerving. He'd rather believe the cowboys were just watching to see if he'd fall on his head. "What about the buck rein?"

"Most of the guys prefer a thicker, tightly braided rein and a full handgrip. But your buck rein is loosely braided and you hold it between your third and fourth fingers."

"You're very observant."

"I know." Her eyes sparkled. "I also noticed that you feed extra rein to the horse when his head drops too low."

"Everybody has their own technique."

"True, but the thick rein is less flexible." She sucked her drink dry. "Beau tried to copy you, but he never got the hang of it. Now you're just stuck in his head."

"I had a little help early on in my career."

"From who?"

"A friend." He didn't want to go into detail about his relationship with Riley Fitzgerald. Vic liked to keep his past private. No one needed to know he'd been raised in one of the most dangerous barrios in Albuquerque.

"Ladies and gentlemen, up next is Beau Billings!" A throng of women screamed the cowboy's name and held up signs with their phone numbers on them. Vic found it amusing that Tanya appeared unfazed by her ex-husband's fan club.

"What?" she asked.

He struggled not to grin. He hadn't been tempted to smile this often in one day let alone one month since he suffered the injury to his face.

"Beau Billings hails from Sierra Vista, Arizona, and right now this cowboy is ranked number sixteen in the country." The announcer's voice echoed through the sound system. It was time for Vic to leave, but he was reluctant to say goodbye—a first for him. Tanya was the only woman in longer than he could remember who appeared relaxed in his company. It would be too easy to let his guard down.

Vic watched Billings prepare for his ride. He paced in front of the chute, his strides short and choppy. The man was nervous. He'd drawn a better bronc than Vic, so his chances of earning a higher score were his for the taking.

"Billings has been paired with Shake Down, a three-year-old gelding from the Dale Anderson Ranch near Big Piney. Let's see if this cowboy can beat Vicario's eighty-nine."

Billings straddled the bronc, and Vic's gaze zeroed in on the buck rein. The cowboy played with his grip and the horse grew nervous in the chute.

"He takes too long," Tanya said. "You take ten seconds max."

Obviously she'd been watching Vic perform for a while. He wasn't sure what to make of that. The chute opened and Shake Down lunged into the arena. The horse landed awkwardly on his front hooves and Billings had to fight from the get-go to keep from being bucked off. The bronc couldn't find its rhythm and Billings's spurring was erratic—the perfect combination for a low score.

The buzzer rang and Billings jumped for safety. "Looks like Shake Down gave our cowboy a run for his money today. Let's see what the judges think." The crowd applauded, but the noise level had dropped noticeably. Rodeo fans knew the difference between a great ride and a mediocre one. Billings's performance had been average at best.

"An eighty-five for Billings! Better luck next time, cowboy!"

Billings spotted Tanya and Vic in the stands and his scowl deepened. As much as Vic enjoyed Tanya's company, it was time to part ways. "Thanks for lunch."

"Sure. See you…somewhere." Her smile was genuine—not flirty.

Good thing or he'd have been tempted to scratch his ride later in Livingston and spend the night in a motel room with Tanya.

TANYA WATCHED VIC'S backside disappear into the crowd. She'd spent thirty-five minutes with him, which was thirty minutes longer than she thought he'd put up with her. Vic was a loner and Beau wasn't the first cowboy to have nothing good to say about him. But Tanya found his quiet personality a nice break from the braggarts on the circuit. And she'd felt a sense of camaraderie with Vic—her competition hadn't exactly welcomed her with open arms, either. They'd given her weird stares and stilted greetings as if they wished she'd remained retired from the sport—not because she was any real threat but because of the attention she and Slingshot drew at the rodeos.

A car accident had ended Tanya's barrel-racing career before she'd been ready to call it quits. She blamed Beau's cheating for robbing her of that last season. It had taken months for her to recover from her injuries and put her failed marriage behind her once she'd signed the divorce papers. Now she was back on the circuit to say a final goodbye to the sport.

"What the hell are you doing with Vicario?" Beau walked—rather limped—toward Tanya.

Ignoring the question, she asked, "Did you sprain your knee?" Beau had been cursed with weak joints to go along with his weak morals.

"Don't change the subject."

Beau didn't love her anymore—if he ever did. But he was a sore loser. He'd fought the divorce tooth and nail, suggesting marriage counseling, but she'd refused. Once a cheater, always a cheater. She made a move to step past him, but he snagged her arm.

"What's with you and Vicario?"

"None of your business."

"The man has ice in his veins, Tanya. You don't know anything about him. Nobody does."

"We're divorced." She planted her hands on her hips. "That means you don't get a say in which men I choose to date, kiss or have sex with."

Beau's jaw dropped and Tanya cringed when she

noticed the attention they'd drawn. Typical Beau—always making a scene.

"When are you and that dumb horse of yours going to call it quits?" Beau's self-esteem grew when he made other people and animals feel worthless. "You and Slingshot are the laughingstock of the circuit."

She'd listened to enough of his crap. Without a word—because Beau hated it when she didn't fight back—she headed to the stock pens to find her stepfather. He intercepted her halfway there.

"Tanya!" Mason Coldwater was in his early sixties and she'd known him since she'd been a young girl. "We need to head home."

"I thought you wanted to stay for the bull riding?" She followed him out to the parking lot and got into his brand-new Lincoln.

"Your horse is causing trouble again." He started the engine and flipped on the air-conditioning.

"What has he done now?" she asked.

"Jumped the damned fence. Took forever for Raymond to catch him. And when he put Slingshot in the barn, the horse kicked the stall door down."

"Next time I'll—"

"There shouldn't be a next time, Tanya." After Mason merged onto the highway, he said, "You're a horse trainer. Not a barrel racer anymore. I need you at the farm. Raymond's not working out."

Raymond Gonzales was the trainer Mason had hired to replace Tanya after she began rodeoing earlier in the year. "Ray has a solid reputation."

"Come back to the farm and help Raymond. Then if

you still want to compete next year, I'll help you choose a decent horse."

It wouldn't matter how many Red Rock horses Mason offered her, he'd find an excuse to bring her back home. She understood his and her mother's fear that she'd injure her leg again. The surgeon had warned that if she broke her left leg again, she might end up walking with a permanent limp. The rehab had been so painful that Tanya hadn't given a thought to competing again until Slingshot had ended up at the farm. The stubborn horse had convinced Tanya that not only did he deserve a second chance to prove himself, but so did she.

Mason paid her a decent salary to train his Appaloosas, and she loved working with the horses. She especially loved the challenge Slingshot presented. It took a month at the farm before the horse's difficult personality became evident, and then Mason had wanted to sell him. Tanya had talked him out of it and had worked tirelessly with the horse, but had made minimal progress. So she'd suggested that Mason allow her to work Slingshot's kinks out on the circuit. Mason had been reluctant, but Tanya had persisted until he caved in.

"Slingshot's getting restless," she said. "He's ready to compete again."

"I think the damned horse doesn't like being separated from you."

"We have a love-hate relationship."

"Maybe you should give him a different name."

Slingshot lived up to his name and then some. He burst out of the alley and broke the barrier like a rock in a slingshot. The only problem was that his momentum made his turns sloppy and he sacrificed valuable seconds getting around the barrels.

"And he's damned ugly," Mason muttered.

The mud-brown horse had no markings, and if you saw him in a lineup with other horses, your gaze would skip over him. But Slingshot had heart—not even Mason could argue with that. The gelding came from a strong bloodline of barrel racers. His legs were straight with no bumps or scars—he hadn't been in any accidents or mishaps—and he possessed a strong back and healthy hooves. Slingshot was built to run, but he was a mystery—just like Victor Vicario—and it was anyone's guess which one would be easier to tame.

Chapter Two

"Ladies and gentlemen, it's time for the women's barrel-racing event at the JUAB County Fairgrounds here in beautiful Nephi, Utah."

Tanya stood with Slingshot, waiting for her turn to enter the alley. She hoped the beast would behave today. She tugged his head lower and whispered in his ear. "Be a sweet boy out there. It's okay if we lose, just don't go rogue on me."

"Hey, Tanya!"

She swallowed a groan. Samantha Martinez, the nineteen-year-old up-and-coming star of barrel racing, entered the line with her horse, Prince Charming. "Have you considered that maybe Slingshot misbehaves because he's suffering from an undiagnosed injury?"

"You wouldn't by chance be accusing me of abusing my horse?"

Samantha's eyes rounded and she sucked in a fake gasp. "Of course not." Then she shrugged her rhinestone shoulders.

What a little snot. A veterinarian had examined

Slingshot and had given him a clean bill of health. The horse's orneriness was all in his head.

"Sometimes it's not the horse but the owner." Samantha smiled. "Maybe Slingshot just doesn't like you."

Tanya's gut coiled in a knot. She'd wondered the same thing but hadn't had the courage to admit it out loud. What if she'd read Slingshot wrong and he didn't want to compete? Hating Samantha for undermining her confidence, she said, "Don't you have a prom to get ready for?"

The cowgirl jerked as if she'd been slapped. Jeez, the girl could dish it out, but she couldn't take it. Tanya regretted snapping at the stuck-up princess, but darn it, her sureness was already lower than the water table in Death Valley.

"You and Slingshot ready?"

Vic stood behind the barrier gate that blocked off one side of the alley. He wasn't smiling—he never did—but his eyes glinted with warmth. Ten days had passed since she last saw him in Wyoming, and not an hour had gone by that he hadn't crossed her mind—sometimes more than once or twice. Dare she hope that he'd thought of her, too?

"I'm ready." She smiled, her heart pumping faster. "But it's always a crapshoot with my horse."

"Did you make a practice run?"

She shook her head. Would he think she was nuts for giving up her time slot earlier in the day? She hadn't wanted to take the chance that Slingshot would injure himself or throw her and knock her out of the competition this afternoon. "We're trying something different."

He didn't comment on her decision, which she appreciated, since she'd already questioned it herself. "You've had a good run so far this month." Who cared if Vic knew she stalked his schedule?

"I've been lucky."

Lucky her fanny. Pure talent had pushed Vic upward in the standings. "You ready to bust your bronc tonight?"

"Yes, ma'am." He winked.

Holy smokes, was Vic flirting with her? Another barrel racer's name was announced and the rider took off down the alley. Tanya was next.

"Good luck." Vic tipped his hat and disappeared.

Tanya pushed the cowboy out of her head and hoisted herself onto Slingshot's back. He stamped his hooves and she patted his neck. "C'mon, big guy. Show Vic what you can do."

"Up next is Tanya McGee from Longmont, Colorado. She and Slingshot need to beat sixteen seconds to take over first place."

Tanya would be happy with twenty-five seconds if Slingshot behaved. The arena attendant signaled and she tapped her boot heels. Then Slingshot raced down the alley and burst through the electronic eye that triggered the timer. They headed straight for the first barrel on the right. With one hand on the saddle horn, she sank deep in her seat, using the reins to guide him. She squeezed his flanks, holding her inside leg securely against his girth, giving him a focal point for the turn. Slingshot executed the turn perfectly and raced in the opposite direction toward the second barrel. She felt him ready himself a second too early and she held on when her leg scraped the barrel, which thankfully remained upright.

To complete the cloverleaf pattern, she and Slingshot raced through the middle toward the rear of the arena, opposite the entrance. Slingshot was going too fast to make the turn and Tanya pulled back on the reins, signaling him to slow up, but the stubborn gelding ignored her and took out the barrel before returning to the alley at an impressive speed.

"Well, folks, if Slingshot hadn't hit that barrel he'd have clocked a time good enough for second place. Too bad a five-second penalty puts Tanya McGee and Slingshot dead last. Better luck next time, cowgirl!"

Tanya hopped off Slingshot. "Good boy." She patted his shoulder, but he jerked his head away as if he knew they'd lost. *Okay, fine. Be a jerk.* She walked him outside the arena past the livestock pens until he cooled down. Then she hitched him to the back of her trailer next to his water and feed. "You rest while I watch Vic."

Tanya had four days to make it to the Rockin' Horse Ranch in Moriarty, New Mexico, for the Women's Professional Rodeo Association barrel-racing event. If Slingshot didn't place in the top three, Mason had warned Tanya, he'd no longer fund her rodeo expenses. She either returned to the farm with Slingshot or paid her own way on the circuit.

With her meager savings, Tanya might be able to compete through the end of July. If Slingshot turned around by then, maybe Mason would give the horse a third chance and pay the cost of their entry fees, gas and lodging for another month or two. She bought a diet cola, found a seat in the shaded section of the grand-stand and waited for the saddle-bronc event to begin.

"Darcy, are you going to the Muggy Rim after the rodeo?"

Tanya eavesdropped on the three buckle bunnies sitting two rows below her. They were a walking advertisement for rodeo bling—rhinestone-studded blouses, belts and boots. Their fake fingernails glittered and even the blush on their cheeks sparkled. When they sat side by side, none of them stood out from the other. What did Beau see in these female zirconias? Didn't the women realize they were being used? No *real* cowboy would bring home all that glitz to meet his mama.

"I don't know," Darcy said.

"If Beau Billings is going, I'm for sure gonna be there." The only brunette in the group spoke.

"Beau is so over you, Sasha. Move on to another cowboy," a dark blonde with purple eye shadow said. "Right, Darcy?"

"You two can fight over Beau," Darcy said. "I want Victor Vicario. I love a mysterious man."

"He scares me," Sasha said. "He never smiles, huh, Heather?"

"Nope and I've always wondered how he got that scar on his face," Heather said.

Darcy fluffed her platinum-blond curls. "There's nothing I like better than a challenge."

Sasha's laugh grated on Tanya's nerves. "If anyone can get Vic's attention, you can, Darcy. I bet you get him into bed on the first try."

Tanya's stomach churned with jealousy and she bit

the inside of her cheek to keep from warning the woman away from Victor.

"Folks, it looks like we're ready to kick off the saddle-bronc competition. We've got a handful of top-notch contenders this afternoon. The first cowboy up is Victor Vicario. Vicario is coming out of the gate on Sidewinder, a two-time national champion bronc."

Tanya ignored the giggles and shouts of the buckle bunnies and focused on Vic as he prepared for his ride. He straddled the bronc and adjusted his grip. Then he looked up into the stands and Tanya sucked in a quick breath. Was he searching for her?

"Oh my God," Darcy said. "He's looking right at me." She waved a poster with her name and phone number in black and pink glitter.

Vic dropped his head, then nodded and the gate swung open. Sidewinder spun wildly, but Vic rode the bronc like a walk in the park. Man and beast danced and sparred to the cheers of the fans. When the buzzer sounded, Vic hung on until he saw an opening and then launched himself at the ground. He hit the dirt, rolled twice and popped to his feet. The crowd went crazy.

"Scar or no scar, he can ride me anytime, any place," Darcy said.

Tanya left the bleachers before she said something to the women that she'd regret. She made her way to the cowboy ready area, her eyes peeled for Vic.

"You looking for me?"

She turned and smiled. "As a matter of fact, I am."

His glance skipped across her face before he locked gazes with her.

"Nice ride," she said.

"Thanks."

An awkward silence settled between them before she asked, "Do you have plans after the rodeo?"

"I ride at eight o'clock in Vernal tonight."

The town was three hours north, and it was only one-thirty in the afternoon. Vic had time to eat before he hit the road. "Want to grab a burger at the Muggy Rim?" If Darcy and her friends saw Vic with Tanya, maybe they'd leave him alone and focus on another un-suspecting cowboy.

"Sure." The tense set of his shoulders relaxed and Tanya read it as a signal that Vic wanted to spend time with her.

"I need to turn Slingshot loose in the corral before we leave. I'll meet you in the parking lot in ten min-utes." Tanya hurried off to take care of her horse, telling herself that the only reason she'd suggested the Muggy Rim was that the bar was close by and not because she wanted to prevent *Darcy* from sneaking off to a motel room for an afternoon quickie with Vic.

VIC TURNED HIS pickup into the gravel lot of the Muggy Rim and parked near the front entrance. The rodeo was still in full swing and the majority of the cowboys and fans wouldn't arrive until after the bull-riding event.

"Have you been here before?" Vic asked, the ques-tion breaking the silence that had accompanied them during the five-minute ride into Nephi.

"Once," she said. "What about you?"

"A few times. Their burgers are good." He got out

of the truck and shut the door, then took a deep breath, hoping the fresh air would clear the lingering scent of Tanya's perfume from his head. The earthy aroma made him think of dark corners, slow music and naked bodies pressing together.

Whoa. This wasn't a date—even though he found her attractive and wouldn't mind getting to know her better. The only reason he'd sought Tanya out at the rodeo was that he was lonely. He'd been lonely a long, long time—by his choice—and he couldn't say for sure what it was about her that had drawn him into the open. No matter, nothing could come of his interest in her, because he couldn't afford any distractions this season. He had too much riding on the line.

He opened the saloon door, and a gust of wind lifted Tanya's hair off her shoulders, the long strands brushing his chest as she stepped past him. A wave of lust gripped his stomach. He'd inhale a burger and then hit the road before he did something stupid like ask her to dance.

"I don't know about you," she said, "but I'm starving." She led the way to a table near the dance floor.

"What can I get you folks to drink?" A waitress wearing a black T-shirt with Muggy Rim printed in white letters across the front stopped at their table.

"I'll take an iced tea," Tanya said.

"Make mine a sweet tea." He'd need the sugar to keep going the rest of the day.

"If you know what you want to eat, I'll put your order in before I get your drinks."

"Sure," Tanya said. "Cheeseburger, hold the onions."

"Fries?" the waitress asked. Tanya shook her head.

"I'll have a double cheeseburger with everything. And fries."

"Comin' right up."

Someone dropped a quarter in the jukebox and a Miranda Lambert song came on. Tanya glanced toward the dance floor, but Vic pretended interest in the baseball game televised on the TV behind the bar.

"I wish I had just a little bit of that winning streak you're running on," she said.

"All winning streaks come to an end eventually." He hoped his streak ended after winning a buckle in Vegas later this year.

"So…" She peeked at him from beneath light brown lashes.

Alarm bells went off inside his head, and the cushioned seat beneath his backside turned to cement.

"Are you seeing anyone?" Her cheeks flushed pink.

"No one steady." *No one period.* He didn't want to give Tanya the idea that he was open to a relationship, but he was curious. "You?"

She shook her head. "Who's got time, right?" A shadow covered her blue eyes. Then she blinked and it disappeared.

"Is your ex making it tough for you to date?" He wasn't an expert on relationships, but he was a guy and he knew firsthand that guys could be jerks.

"Not in the way you mean." She opened her mouth to explain, but the waitress appeared with their drinks.

"Food should be up in ten minutes."

Against his better judgment, Vic prompted Tanya to

confide in him. "I'm a good listener if you want someone to unload on."

"I don't want to bore you with the details."

"Nothing about you is boring." *Damn*. Like an inexperienced poker player, he'd just shown his hand. Tanya was too easy to talk to and he hadn't had a meaningful conversation with anyone in months. Each day he spoke to numerous people—convenience-store clerks, rodeo personnel and waitresses—but they were just words.

"Beau said he'd always dreamed of marrying the girl next door." She sipped her tea. "Then after I caught him cheating—which I later came to find out was actually the fourth buckle bunny he'd slept with behind my back—he admitted that I wasn't exciting enough for him." She snorted.

Holy hell. Beau Billings was a bigger fool than Vic first believed. Tanya McGee didn't have a buckle bunny body, but that didn't make her any less hot in Vic's eyes. "His loss."

"Thanks." She blew out a soft sigh. "Beau's a sore loser. At first he tried to talk me out of filing for a divorce, insisting we should start a family. That being a father would keep him grounded."

Family. The word made Vic nauseated. His only brother died years ago, killed by police during an armed robbery. Vic's older sister by one year had committed suicide after she was raped by a gangbanger and discovered she was pregnant. His younger sister by ten years had gotten pregnant at seventeen and ended up in jail for prostitution, leaving his mother with custody of her only grandson. "Do you want kids?"

"Not with Beau, that's for sure." Her gaze softened. "But yes, someday I'd like to have a family of my own."

Vic didn't care to talk about family—he hadn't had a good experience with his. "I thought Slingshot might come through for you this afternoon. That horse can run."

"I'm not crazy for thinking Slingshot has it in him to win, right?"

"Maybe after a year of competition he'll get his legs under him."

"I wish I had that long," she said.

"What do you mean?"

Tanya nodded to the waitress heading their way with the food. After they were left alone, she said, "If I don't win in New Mexico, my stepfather's pulling his support. But I'm not ready to give up on Slingshot yet."

"Then keep competing." He bit into his burger, taking a small bite so his chewing wouldn't distort his face, not that Tanya ever stared at his scar—it was as if she couldn't see the puckered flesh dissecting his cheek.

"Easy for you to say when you place in the money at every event." She waved a hand before her face. "I'm not throwing in the towel yet. I have enough in savings to last through the end of the month if we don't win next time."

"What did you do between your divorce and returning to the circuit?"

"I train Mason's Appaloosas." She snuck one of his fries and dipped it into the circle of ketchup he'd poured on his plate. "I consider myself a good trainer, but every technique I've tried with Slingshot has backfired." She swallowed another bite, then said, "I worry that it's me. That Slingshot doesn't want *me* riding him."

"Why do you think that?"

"He's the first horse I've competed on that someone else worked with first." A tiny wrinkle appeared between her eyebrows. "Maybe he's still attached to his previous trainer."

Vic checked his cell phone. He still had plenty of time to get to the Dinosaur Roundup Rodeo. "Where in New Mexico are you and Slingshot headed?"

"Moriarty for the WPRA barrel-racing event. What's next after Vernal for you?"

"Steamboat Springs, Colorado, tomorrow afternoon, then Laramie, Wyoming, that night."

"July's a busy rodeo month, but what do you normally do between competitions the rest of the year?"

"Rest." Vic used to spend time with Riley and Maria Fitzgerald at the Juan Alvarez Ranch for Boys in New Mexico, but when they hired Cruz as a wrangler after he got out of prison, Vic hadn't had the guts to visit. Instead he hid out in cheap motel rooms and surfed the web or read the stash of books he carried on the road with him.

The bar was filling up. If he left now, he could catch a catnap in his truck before his next ride.

"Vic?"

He swung his gaze to Tanya.

"Ask me." She tilted her head toward the dance floor. He shouldn't.

She smiled. "It's just a dance."

What could it hurt? One dance and then he'd leave. He stood and held out his hand. Her fingers slid across his palm and he fought the urge to hold her prisoner and never let her go. He found an open spot on the floor and Tanya snuggled close as if they were regular dance partners—make that lovers.

He placed his hand against her lower back and she pressed her palm to his chest. The floor was too crowded to move more than a few inches in any direction, so they stood in place, their hips swaying...bumping and oh man. Tanya's warm body and soft curves put his willpower to the test. If he closed his eyes he could imagine they were alone in a dark room instead of standing in a crowd of sweaty bodies.

"It's been forever since I've danced." Tanya's confession ignited a slow burn inside him. He tightened his arms around her. She felt small and vulnerable, which made it all the more impressive that she could handle a horse like Slingshot.

"Have you ever been married, Vic?"

"No, ma'am."

"Never came close?"

"Nope."

Her fingertip touched his cheek and he jumped inside. "Is it because of the scar?" She leaned back and looked him in the eye.

He admired Tanya for asking such a direct question. "I've never given much thought to the future." Marriage had never been on his radar. Since he'd been nineteen he'd had one goal—winning a national title. He couldn't move forward with his life until he put the past behind him.

"Mind if I cut in?" a feminine voice interrupted them.

Tanya stiffened in Vic's arms a second before she smashed her breasts against his chest. The feel of her sent a rush of blood straight to his crotch. Then she bumped her pelvis—intentionally—against his erection before acknowledging the interruption.

"I'm Darcy." The buxom blonde batted her butterfly lashes.

Vic opened his mouth to decline Darcy's offer, but Tanya beat him to it. "No can do, Darcy." Tanya's fingers bit into his arm. "We were just leaving." She stared at him. "Right, Vic?"

Tanya's eyes flashed—from anger or desire, it didn't matter. He was leaving the bar with her. "We're out of here."

Tanya stepped forward, but Darcy blocked her path. "Where are you leaving to…if I may ask?"

Tanya slid her arm through Vic's. "Somewhere more private."

Darcy's eyes widened. "You two are sleeping together?"

Vic waited for Tanya to set Darcy straight, but instead of denying the accusation, she dragged him through the crowd and straight out the door.

After they got into the pickup, she spoke. "Vic?"

He stared out the windshield afraid to look at her. Afraid to see in her eyes the same yearning he was positive showed in his. "What?" He forced the word past his lips.

"I know you have another ride tonight, but I'm going to ask anyway."

He stopped breathing.

"Do you want to get a motel room with me?"

Chapter Three

There were a thousand reasons why he and Tanya shouldn't get a motel room —the most important being that he had another go-round waiting for him in Vernal. But when he stared into her blue eyes, he couldn't remember why that ride was important. He started the engine and drove three miles to an out-of-the way motel no other cowboys would stay at for the night.

When he pulled up in front of the office of the Sweet Dreams Inn, there was only one other customer—a red Mustang parked outside room 7. He'd ask Tanya one more time, hoping mostly for his sake that she'd change her mind. But before he voiced the question, she'd opened her door and with one boot on the pavement she said, "You're not having second thoughts, are you?"

Nothing short of a bullet through the heart would stop him now. "You want to wait here while I register for a room?" Tanya wasn't like other women he'd shared a motel bed with. She might care if someone recognized her. Thanks to her ex-husband's wild ways, she'd already been the victim of gossip, and he didn't want people talking bad about her because of him.

She shook her head and got out, then came around the hood and slipped her fingers through his. "I'll go in with you."

Five minutes later the motel manager handed Vic a plastic key card with the number 4 on it. The walk to the room took ten seconds. His attraction to Tanya convinced him the sex would be great—better than great—but it was what happened after they made love that worried Vic. This could only be a one-night stand. He couldn't afford to lose focus on his goal, and it would be too easy to become preoccupied with Tanya. He slid the card through the lock and opened the door.

The king-size bed beckoned, but his boots sank into the sidewalk as if it were made of wet concrete. Tanya's fingers squeezed his right biceps and then she stood on tiptoe and pressed a kiss against his neck. Her warm breath puffed across his skin, propelling him forward. He shut the door behind them and flipped the locks.

He didn't bother with the lights.

A HEAVY WARMTH pressing against her backside woke Tanya. It took a fraction of a second for her to remember she was at the Sweet Dreams Inn with Vic. The room was pitch-black, only a sliver of light spilled beneath the closed bathroom door. She'd asked Vic to turn on the bedside lamp after they tumbled naked onto the mattress—she'd wanted to gawk at every inch of muscle—but he'd distracted her with kisses and touches and she'd lost herself in their lovemaking.

She'd seen through his tough act. He wanted her and others to believe he wasn't self-conscious about the scar on his face, but he was. If he didn't care about it, he'd smile and laugh and not stop himself when the action stretched the puckered flesh, pulling one side of his mouth down.

She made a conscious effort to look him in the eye when they talked, but it was difficult to ignore the ugly mark. She could only imagine how painful the wound had been, but was reluctant to ask how he'd gotten it for fear he'd push her away for good.

Vic stirred, his hand moving from her belly to her breast. His thumb flicked her nipple and she exhaled a soft sigh.

"If I tell you something," she whispered into the dark, "promise you won't get a big head?"

He pressed his mouth to her neck and nibbled her skin. "Promise."

"On second thought, never mind."

He sat up and rolled her onto her back. She could only make out the shadow of his face as he loomed over her. "You can't leave a man hanging like that."

She wished she could see his eyes. "Rodeo's already given you a big ego."

"If that's the way you feel, then…" His mouth trailed kisses down her neck, across her collarbone, then lower…lower… Her back arched and she moaned. She knew it was wrong to think of her ex when she was in bed with Vic, but Beau had never spent much time pleasuring her, and Vic acted as if he couldn't get enough of her. The sensations he aroused in her were powerful and humbling.

He kissed his way up her body and then brushed the

hair from her eyes. "What we're you going to tell me a few minutes ago?"

"I can't remember." She curled against him.

"Guess I'll have to do this all over again." His mouth latched onto her breast.

"Wait," she cried out in defeat. "I haven't caught my breath yet." She could feel his smile against her stomach. "Okay, fine. You're amazing in bed."

"Amazing? That's it?"

He kissed her—a tender caress that led to more kisses on her nose, cheeks and forehead. This gentle side of Vic was a surprise and she savored every touch and whispered word.

"My turn." She pushed him off her.

A silent chuckle rumbled through his chest, but it didn't last long.

VIC WOKE AT 6:00 a.m. to snoring sounds coming from the other side of the bed. Tanya rested on her back, her arms and legs spread wide as if she'd been making snow angels on the mattress. Watching her filled him with longing. He'd missed his ride in Vernal last night but being with Tanya had meant more to him than winning his next rodeo. More than was good for his sanity. Tanya was an easy woman to be with and the first woman in forever he could be himself with.

But the timing was wrong. Hell, the timing might never be right. Once he won the national championship buckle later this year, he'd retire from rodeo. Tanya only knew him as a broncbuster. When he hung up his spurs for good, she might not care for the new Vic—whoever he turned out to be. He'd be a fool to lose his heart to her when he'd end up disappointing her down the road.

This was the end of the line for them. And as much as he wanted to make love to her again before he drove her to the fairgrounds to pick up Slingshot, he didn't dare. Tanya had already worked her way beneath his skin, and it wouldn't take a whole lot of effort on her part to blaze a trail straight to his heart. Thank God he had a lot of rodeos and a lot of miles ahead of him to shake off her memory.

He slipped from the bed, covered Tanya with the sheet, then took a shower and threw on a clean pair of jeans and a T-shirt. After tugging on his socks and boots, he stepped outside to check his phone messages—three voice mails from Maria Fitzgerald. An uneasy feeling crawled up his spine. This couldn't be good news.

"It's Maria, Victor. Call me as soon as you get this message. And I don't care what time it is."

"It's Maria again. Please call me. It's important."

"Victor, if you don't call me soon, I'll send Riley looking for you."

Damn it, he should have checked his messages before they left the Muggy Rim. He pressed the number 6 on his speed dial. Maria answered on the first ring.

"Are you driving?" she asked.

"I'm standing next to my truck. What's going on, Maria?"

"I have bad news."

Vic's mind raced through the people employed at

the boys' ranch and wondered who had been hurt or who was ill.

"Judge Hamel contacted me yesterday. Evidently I'm the only one who has your cell number."

"What's the bad news?"

"It concerns your nephew, Alex."

Vic had never met his twenty-one-year-old sister Natalia's son. He hadn't set foot in Albuquerque in over six years. The last time he'd spoken to his mother—maybe seven months ago—she had custody of Alex because Natalia was sitting in prison convicted of prostitution. "What happened?"

"A neighbor found Alex wandering around the parking lot at night in the apartment complex where he and your mother live. Vic, your mother's gone. Vanished. The police have no idea what happened to her. They think she might have been abducted."

Abducted? *Yeah, right.* Vic's legs grew weak and he locked his knees. He knew what had happened to his mother. She'd left Alex to go buy drugs and had probably gotten high and never returned to the apartment. Or maybe she'd overdosed and was lying on a dirty mattress in some abandoned house in the barrio.

Vic's head spun and he slid down the side of the truck until his butt hit the asphalt. His gut twisted with anger and resentment as he envisioned his mother shooting up heroin or smoking crystal meth until she passed out. "Where's Alex now?" The nephew he'd yet to meet must be terrified.

"The New Mexico Children, Youth and Families Department placed him in a state-run facility while they search for your mother. But, Vic?"

"What?"

"Judge Hamel said even if they find her, Alex won't be allowed to live with her anymore."

"Where will he go?" Natalia had had over a year left on her sentence.

"Judge Hamel isn't sure, but she suggested it would be best if you returned to Albuquerque and took temporary custody of Alex. He's too young to be in a group home with older kids, but they have no other option right now."

"Custody?" Exactly what did that word entail?

"I know rodeo is important, but Alex needs you."

"Alex doesn't even know me, Maria." As for rodeo, hell yes, it was important. No one but him knew the real reason he'd committed himself to the sport all these years. He'd come too far now to walk away.

"You're all the family Alex has left."

"What am I supposed to do with a four-year-old?"

"He's almost five."

Hell, he couldn't even remember his nephew's birthday. "There's no way they'll grant me custody of a kid that age. I'm on the road every day and I live out of motel rooms and my pickup."

"Temporary custody, Vic. Only until they find a better place for Alex." After a short pause Maria said, "Judge Hamel has already vouched for you. CYFD is waiting for you to pick up Alex."

Vic glanced longingly at the motel door, wishing he could crawl into bed with Tanya and forget all the ugliness that existed in the world—his world. He closed his eyes, and his mother's face flashed through his mind. She'd brought him into the world and she'd made him pay for it every day. He believed he'd finally put her and the barrio behind him for good, but her drug addiction was a stark reminder that he could never outrun who he was.

"Come to the ranch," Maria said. "Riley surprised me with a trip to Hawaii and we leave tomorrow, but you and Alex are welcome to stay in the main house. Alex will enjoy playing with the twins and Cruz's daughter, Dani."

Vic had a string of rodeos he needed to compete in to pad his earnings and secure a spot in this year's NFR. As for bunking down at Maria and Riley's place—no way.

"Judge Hamel's working with CYFD to find Alex a home by the end of August at the latest."

"Alex will have to come on the road with me." Vic's mother had made his life miserable for so long, and he refused to let her latest drug relapse rob him of his goal.

"If you're determined to keep rodeoing, then drop Alex off here. I'm sure Cruz's wife, Sara, will be happy to look after him until Riley and I return."

Sara might be fine with the arrangement, but he doubted Cruz would approve—not after Vic's family had brought him nothing but trouble. "I can swing it if it's only for a few weeks," he said.

"I'm glad to hear you say that. I knew you'd do the right thing."

Doing the right thing should help Vic feel better, but

all it did was make him detest his mother more. "Where do I find Alex?"

"When you arrive in Albuquerque, call Judge Hamel and she'll give you the address of the group home where Alex is staying. I'll text you Judge Hamel's number in case you don't have it."

"Sure."

"Victor?"

"What?"

"Judge Hamel said she'd let me know when and where they find your mother."

Right now he couldn't care less if they ever found his mother. "Thanks."

"I'm sorry, Vic."

He disconnected the call. A few seconds later his phone beeped with a text message—Judge Hamel's phone number.

He glanced between the room door and his phone. He wanted so badly to stay with Tanya. Maybe it was a good thing he'd gotten the call now about Alex. At least he could walk away from her, before all his problems caused her grief. He climbed to his feet and went to the motel office, where he paid for another day—in case Tanya didn't wake up before the checkout time.

Then he returned to the room and fumbled his way in the dark to the nightstand, where he scribbled a note on the pad of paper and left it along with fifty dollars in cash to catch a cab to the fairgrounds. This wasn't how he wanted to part ways with Tanya, but maybe it was best she learn now that she was better off without him.

He set the key card next to the note, turned the lock on the door and left.

TANYA GOT OUT of the cab behind the fairgrounds near the livestock pens. Most of the animals had been loaded and hauled off except for a handful of horses used by the rodeo workers. She paid the driver, then shut the door and went over to the corral where Slingshot munched on hay. He didn't look her way when she called his name. Go figure—he hadn't missed her at all.

"About time you showed up to get your horse." A man walked out from behind a flatbed trailer loaded with leftover hay bales from the rodeo.

"I had some business to take care of," she said, refusing to think about Victor abandoning her at the Sweet Dreams Inn. The cab fare he'd left for her was a slap in the face.

"I'll get him loaded ASAP." She walked across the lot, each step pounding into the pavement harder than the previous. She'd never been more humiliated and hurt in her life. When would she learn that rodeo cowboys were all the same? The bigheaded lugs only cared about their next ride.

She'd been a fool to believe last night had meant anything to Vic. That *she'd* meant something to him. She hopped into her pickup, then backed up to the corral gate and opened the trailer doors. "Mind if I take a few of those bales off your hands?" It would save her time if she didn't have to stop at a feed store. Besides, the sooner she left Utah, the better.

"Take as much as you want. The rest is going to the humane society." He motioned to Slingshot. "You need help?"

"No, thanks." She entered the corral. "C'mon, big

guy." She took his lead rope, surprised when he followed without protest. Once he was secure in his trailer stall and she'd loaded the hay, Tanya took off.

Moriarty, New Mexico, was ten hours away and she had two days to get there. She'd contacted a mobile-home park weeks ago and received permission to use one of their pads to park the truck and horse trailer. They had public showers, free Wi-Fi, a washateria and, according to the owner, an acre of grass for Slingshot. The daily rate was more than she'd budgeted, but she needed to do her laundry.

If the camping site was a hellhole, then she'd call one of her stepfather's friends in the area and ask if she could camp out on their property for a day or two. She was nothing if not organized and she'd mapped out an entire season of rodeos after the first of the year. But the one thing she hadn't planned on was Victor Vicario taking off on her before she woke up.

She hadn't gone to the motel room with him expecting anything to come of their night, but she'd held out hope their time together might turn into a… *Relationship* wasn't the right word, because Vic was a loner. Fling maybe? She and Victor were bound to cross paths from time to time the remainder of the summer and she'd hoped they'd become friends   friends with benefits. She hadn't realized how lonely she'd been since she joined the circuit.

For the millionth time she went over the events of last night in her head but couldn't figure out what she'd done or hadn't done that had caused Vic to bolt without saying goodbye.

Maybe he was worried you'd make last night out to be more than just sex.

She couldn't remember every word they'd whispered to each other in the dark, but she was certain she'd never uttered anything threatening like *I love you*.

Her brain told her to move on, but her heart wasn't ready to give up hope. There had to be a reason he left in a hurry, but they didn't exchange phone numbers, so she had no way of getting in touch with him. Maybe it was best if they didn't run into each other for a while. By the time they crossed paths again, she might be ready for his apology.

"THANK YOU FOR getting here as soon as you could, Mr. Vicario," Renee Leonard said as she searched through the folders on the desk.

He would have arrived an hour ago if he hadn't first had to stop by the police station and speak with the cop investigating his mother's disappearance. Officer Darrel Andrews claimed a neighbor phoned 911 at 10:00 p.m. to report a little boy walking alone in the parking lot. When the cops arrived, they discovered his mother's apartment door wide-open. There were no signs of a robbery and Officer Andrews believed Vic's mother might have taken off sometime the day before, but Alex wasn't talking to anyone. Vic wasn't surprised his nephew refrained from speaking—the kid must have been terrified at being left alone in the apartment.

Andrews said he'd be in touch as soon as they had any new information, but considering his mother's history of drug abuse, it was anyone's guess what had happened to her. He shouldn't even think it, but the thought crossed his mind anyway—it was probably better for Alex if his grandmother was never found.

"Before I have Martha bring Alex into my office," Renee said, "I wanted to go over a few things with you. Are you considering applying for legal custody of Alex?"

Legal custody? "No." Vic had nothing to offer a kid like Alex. He'd step up and do his duty until they found a proper foster home for his nephew but nothing more.

"Alex is experiencing a lot of different emotions and you shouldn't take his actions or reactions to you personally. Just let him express himself however he feels comfortable. In a few weeks you need to get him to a therapist who will help him process his feelings. I'm sure he's wondering where his grandmother is and why she left him."

This sounded like a lot more than just babysitting the kid for a short while.

"If you're worried about the cost of therapy, the state will cover his sessions. There's a clinic that works with children right down the street from here." Renee handed him a business card.

"Alex's birthday is September twenty-seventh, which is past the cutoff date to enroll him in kindergarten for the fall. He'll need to wait one more year before he goes to school. There are lots of pre-K programs he could attend and we can help you find one. It's important that he socialize with other kids."

Renee had no clue what Vic's life was like or that he

was too busy chasing a title to socialize himself. Maybe the woman thought rodeo was Vic's hobby.

"These are Alex's medical records." She handed Vic the paperwork. "A list of his immunizations. He had a checkup with a pediatrician two days ago and the doctor said there's no physical reason for Alex not to be speaking." Renee picked up a kid's backpack from the floor by her chair and handed it to Vic. "Some clothes, a few books and parenting pamphlets that might be of help."

The only thing of use to Vic right now was finding a home for his nephew.

Renee texted on her phone and a moment later another woman walked into her office. "Martha," Renee said. "This is Alex's uncle, Victor Vicario. Victor, Martha is in charge of the group home Alex was placed in."

Vic caught the wince Martha tried to conceal when she saw his scar. "I'm sure Renee told you that Alex hasn't said a word since he was brought to the group home. Several of the children have tried to engage him in conversation, but he ignores them."

Poor kid.

"He doesn't eat a lot and he's underweight for his age, so be sure to offer him snacks between meals. He may not tell you he's hungry, but you should encourage him to eat."

"How has he been sleeping?" Renee asked.

"He hasn't woken with nightmares. But if he does, just reassure him the best you can. He's not combative and he doesn't pick fights with the other kids but…" Martha rubbed her brow.

"What?" Vic asked.

"He stares out the window all day yet refuses to go outside and join the other kids in the yard."

Was Alex waiting for his grandmother to come get him? Vic began to sweat. He wanted to help his nephew, but the kid deserved better than an uncle he'd never met and spending most of his day in a pickup. Alex needed specialized help—help Vic wasn't qualified to give him. He looked at Renee. "How long did you say it will take to find him a permanent foster home?"

"Foster homes are never permanent. We have good people who sign up to take children in, but life is full of unexpected surprises and sometimes they have to send the child back to us. We're hoping that this won't be the case for Alex. He needs stability in his life right now, but we can't guarantee him that."

"What if Alex doesn't want to be with me?"

"If you have issues with Alex, feel free to contact me. I'll notify you as soon as a foster home opens up for him."

Renee's expression appeared sincere and Vic had no reason to believe she wouldn't do her best to find a solution to Alex's living situation.

"Judge Hamel gave me the Fitzgeralds' phone number and said you'd be staying there with Alex until you decide what to do about your rodeo schedule."

They'd been told what he did for a living, but it sounded as if Judge Hamel had fudged the story. He wanted to make sure these women knew the truth. "I don't think you understand," he said.

"Here's Alex." Martha opened the door wider. "You

must have grown tired of waiting for us adults to finish talking."

Vic shifted in his chair and his heart clenched when he saw his nephew. He looked like Natalia when she'd been his age. Vic was ten years older than his sister and he felt a prick of shame that this was the first time he was meeting his nephew.

Big brown eyes stared at Vic. The kid appeared afraid of him—then Vic remembered his scar. Damn, what the hell was he supposed to do about that? He got up from the chair and went down on one knee in front of the boy. "It looks a lot worse than it really is." He smiled, then straightened his mouth when Alex's eyes widened.

"I'm your uncle Vic. Your mom was my sister. You ready to hang out with me for a few weeks?"

The boy's eyes remained glued to Vic's scar. Alex didn't act as though he wanted to go with his uncle— maybe Vic could wiggle his way out of this tight spot.

"Alex, it's going to take time to find a family for you to live with. Do you want to stay here at the home or would you like to go with your uncle?" Renee asked.

The room held its breath, waiting for the boy to make his decision. Then Alex pointed a tiny finger at Vic, sealing his uncle's fate.

Chapter Four

"Ladies and gentlemen, up next is a cowgirl from Longmont, Colorado. Tanya McGee and her horse Slingshot
need a time of fourteen seconds or better to take home
a trophy tonight."

"You can do this, Slingshot," Tanya whispered in
the horse's ear. "If you don't win, we're done." And
Tanya didn't want this to be her last ride. She wanted to
walk away from barrel racing with at least one win—
a positive memory to replace the car accident that had
abruptly ended her career. "I'm warning you, Slingshot,
your life at Red Rock will be boring."

Slingshot loved to race barrels. She felt it in her
bones. If he didn't like to compete he'd balk at being
hauled from state to state, but he was a good traveler. He
never gave her trouble loading or standing in the trailer.
His only weakness was not responding to her com-
mands during competition, and she didn't know why.

"Be sure to stick around after the rodeo, folks.
Tonight's cowgirls will be signing autographs at the
front entrance."

Tanya climbed into the saddle and took several deep

breaths, then closed her eyes, but they popped opened when an image of Victor's face flashed through her mind. The past two days she'd convinced herself that their night at the motel had meant nothing. The fact that Vic's face remained clear in her memory stung. Slingshot tensed and she relaxed her leg muscles. This might be her last race with the horse and she didn't need Vic's ghost sabotaging her ride.

"Looks like Tanya and Slingshot have entered the alley and are ready to go."

As soon as she was given the signal, Tanya clicked her heels and Slingshot bolted. He broke the electronic barrier at full speed, then rounded the first barrel with ease. This time felt different—this time they were going to win. Slingshot made a tight turn around the second barrel and picked up speed. He was going too fast and she feared he'd take out the third barrel and injure them both, so she reined him in—too much. Slingshot's muscles tensed as he came out of the turn and they lost valuable seconds before he made it back to the alley.

"Tanya McGee and Slingshot posted 14.9 seconds! Good enough for second place. Thank you for coming out tonight and supporting our WPRA sanctioned barrel-racing event in Moriarty. Drive safe."

Tanya rode Slingshot out of the arena and then walked him for ten minutes before turning him loose in the holding pen. "You threw that race." Slingshot ignored her and drank from the water tank. "You know you're capable of winning." When he lifted his head and snorted, she asked, "Is it me? You just don't like me riding you?"

His brown eyes blinked at her; then he turned his back and joined the other horses at the feeder. She left him to rest and went to sign autographs. The money she won tonight would pay for one more entry fee, but she'd depleted her savings. From here on out, if she decided to continue competing she'd have to put all her expenses on a credit card.

Is it worth it?

That was the million-dollar question.

"Great ride, Tanya." Debbie Winters, the first-place winner, patted the seat next to her at the signing table.

Tanya didn't like Debbie. The former Miss Rodeo Queen was beautiful, talented and spoiled. And she'd slept with Beau—after Tanya had filed for divorce. But still...

"Beau's concerned about you," Debbie said.

"I doubt that." Beau didn't care about anyone but himself.

"He said you're chasing after Victor Vicario."

Chasing?

Debbie smiled at the young girl who shoved a program in her face. "I know you're upset things didn't work out with Beau, but did you seriously think they would?" She returned the program to the little girl. "You're not the right woman for him."

Tanya waited for her turn to sign the program, but the girl walked off. "And I suppose you're the right woman for him?"

Debbie flashed a smile. "Do you still have feelings for Beau? Because if you think there's a chance of you two getting back together, then—"

"No way. I'm over him. It's only his ego talking when he tells people that I'm not."

"Then the rumors are true—you hooked up with Victor Vicario?"

"Hooked up?" Had someone spotted Vic's truck parked outside the Sweet Dreams Inn?

"Darcy Kimble saw you two leave the Muggy Rim together."

"We grabbed a bite to eat, so what?" Damn Darcy and her big mouth.

"But you left your horse at the fairgrounds overnight." Debbie wiggled her eyebrows.

"I don't see that this is any of your business." Tanya wiped her perspiring brow.

"Beau's worried that you're desperate and that's why you're with Victor."

Tanya clenched her jaw until her anger subsided. "First of all, I'm not desperate. And second, I'm not *with* anyone."

"Just the same, you should be careful around Victor. You shouldn't trust a man who has no friends."

"How do you know he doesn't have any friends?" Tanya asked.

"Beau said he never socializes with the other cowboys."

"Since when is Beau Billings an expert on other people's lives? He's jealous because Vic's one of the best saddle-bronc riders on the circuit."

And Vic was just as good in bed. Tanya's body heated when she recalled the things he'd done to her with his hands and mouth. Beau's lovemaking paled in comparison to what she and Vic had shared, partly because Vic had made sure she enjoyed the experience. Beau believed a woman should just be grateful to have him in her bed and he didn't see any reason to go out of his way to please her.

Tanya nudged Debbie. "Why all the questions?"

Debbie's cheeks reddened, but she waited to answer until after she signed a program for a pair of sisters. "I needed to know if it's really over between you and Beau."

"You seriously like him, don't you?"

"Yes." She lifted her chin. "I think he's misunderstood is all."

Misunderstood? Tanya laughed. It was all an act. She wanted to warn Debbie but doubted she'd listen. With Beau's good looks and Debbie's beauty… "You two would make beautiful babies."

Debbie's eyes lit up. "I know, right?"

Debbie and Beau's big egos deserved each other. "If you want Beau, go after him."

"You're sure you don't have any lingering feelings for him?"

Not any lovey-dovey feelings, that was for sure. "I'm totally over Beau." Tanya got the impression that Debbie was looking for a reason not to pursue Beau, because she knew he was a lost cause. Too bad some women didn't know when to call it quits.

Debbie shoved her chair back and stood. "See you down the road."

Maybe Tanya and the beauty queen had something in common after all—whether it was a man or a horse, neither of them knew when to back off. Tanya walked back to the livestock pens. "Slingshot!" He swung his head in her direction. "I'm giving you one more chance."

Because Slingshot deserved to prove he could win and because Tanya wasn't ready to say goodbye to Vic.

"I'M GETTING HUNGRY," Vic said. "You want to grab lunch somewhere, Alex?"

His nephew stared in a trancelike state from the backseat. The kid had been silent since they left Albuquerque. The social worker had made sure Vic knew how to secure the booster seat in the back of his pickup. She said Alex was small for his age—barely thirty pounds and thirty-eight inches tall—and that he'd need to use the booster until he gained more weight.

"You like burgers? Tacos? Chicken fingers?" He didn't expect an answer, but he glanced in the rearview mirror, hoping for some kind of reaction. Nothing.

He could only guess what was going through the boy's head—none of it good. He took the next exit off the highway and pulled into a truck stop with a fast food restaurant inside. He filled the pickup with gas and parked in front of the building.

"Let's see what they have in here to eat." He helped Alex out of the booster seat and set him on the ground. "Do you need to use the restroom?" No answer. They entered the convenience store, where he guided Alex into the men's restroom. Vic stepped up to a urinal and relieved himself. Alex just stared at the urinals. "Guess you can't reach that high yet." He opened a stall door. "This will work better." Vic held the door partially closed in case Alex needed his help. After a couple of minutes he heard the toilet flush. When Alex stepped out of the stall, Vic held him over the sink and helped him wash his hands. They shared a dryer, then left the restroom. In the adjoining restaurant Vic ordered a hamburger for himself and chicken fingers for Alex along with two sodas, then changed his mind. "Make one of those a Hi-C drink."

"We have milk," the cashier said.

"Milk sounds even better." Vic carried the tray of food to a booth and sat across from Alex. The boy's chin barely cleared the edge of the table.

"Dig in." Vic took a bite of his burger.

Tiny fingers picked off pieces of the chicken and popped them into his mouth. Vic pushed his fries across the tray. "Help yourself." He opened a ketchup packet and squeezed a blob on the food wrapper, then dunked the end of a fry in it. Alex copied him. Now he knew two things about Alex—he liked chicken and ketchup on his fries.

"You been to any movies lately?" Alex shook his head. Good, Vic was making progress. "Me, neither. Do you have a favorite football team?" Stupid question. He doubted the boy knew anything about sports when he'd been raised around females his whole life. Vic's older brother had played football in middle school but got mixed up with gangs and dropped out of school in tenth grade.

Vic hadn't tried out for sports in school. Maybe if he'd had any discipline in his early life, he might have been able to handle a coach yelling at him, but he'd gotten enough flak from his teachers and didn't need more after school let out. "I cheer for the Dallas Cowboys when I can catch a game in my motel room."

He wanted to learn as much as possible about Alex, but what if his questions spawned bad memories? The last thing he intended to do was make his nephew cry. Then again maybe Alex was too tough to cry. Vic and his siblings had learned early in life that crying got them nowhere with their mother. Surely Vic's mother had treated Alex the same way. Why else would she have gone off and left Alex alone? Hell, she'd probably forgotten her grandson even lived with her. Vic knew from experience that when she needed a hit, everyone around her ceased to exist.

"Did I tell you that I rode a horse called Banjo once?" He took a sip of his soda. "He was pitch-black with white markings on his legs. Looked like he wore socks."

Alex's gaze remained glued to his food, but Vic sensed he was listening because when he'd pause, Alex would glance up at Vic as if he was waiting for his uncle to continue speaking.

"I think you're gonna like rodeo. You ever met a real cowboy before?" Vic didn't consider himself a real cowboy. He wasn't born and raised on a ranch or a farm. He knew nothing about caring for or training horses. He just rode the wild ones. "You have to be careful around the rough stock because they can get agitated."

Vic ate the rest of his burger, but Alex had only eaten two of his four chicken fingers. "If you finish your meal, you can buy a treat before we hit the road again."

Alex inhaled his chicken. Evidently the kid liked

sweets. "Good job, buddy. You have to eat all your meals, so you'll grow up nice and strong. Who knows, maybe one day you'll be a bull rider." He gathered their garbage and dumped the contents into the trash container. "Let's check out the ice cream in the freezer." They returned to the convenience mart and stared at the treats in the freezer. "Which one do you want?" Vic asked.

Alex glanced at Vic, then back at the freezer. "You want me to lift you up?" The knot in his gut eased when Alex raised his arms. Vic hoisted him higher so he could view his choices. "Take whichever one you want."

He picked a firecracker Popsicle and Vic said, "Grab another for me. I haven't had one of these since I was a kid." Ice-cream trucks didn't dare drive through the barrio unless they wanted to risk being robbed at gunpoint.

Back in his pickup, Vic set Alex in the front seat next to him and they ate their treats in silence. He waited for the boy to finish, then wiped off his sticky hands with a napkin. When pieces of the tissue stuck to his fingers, Vic said, "We better buy a few supplies before we take off."

They returned to the store and Vic carried a shopping basket through the aisles, Alex following behind him. He dropped a box of tissues in the basket then a package of wet wipes, granola bars, bubble gum, a six-pack of water bottles, a notepad and a package of colored markers.

Back in the truck, Vic buckled Alex into the booster seat and cleaned his sticky hands with a wipe. "We have a lot of driving to do, so if you get bored you can color." He set the markers and pad of paper on the seat next to Alex.

Once he merged onto the highway, Vic tuned the radio to a sports talk show. He checked the rearview mirror every few minutes. Alex stared out the window, his face expressionless. Vic wished he knew how to reassure the kid that everything would be okay. But Vic wasn't sure anything would be okay again.

"If you ask me, rodeos are pretty awesome." He hoped the one-sided conversation would keep the boy's bad memories at bay. Vic could manage that when Alex was awake, but he had no idea how to protect him from bad dreams when he slept.

"We'll arrive at the rodeo early this Saturday and then I'll show you around." He checked the mirror again—Alex had fallen asleep.

What kind of mother had his sister been—besides not a good one? The social worker had no idea who Alex's father was—there was no record of Natalia receiving any child support payments. The guy was probably a gangbanger or had been one of her paying customers. He gripped the wheel tighter. If Maria Fitzgerald hadn't taken Vic under her wings, he might be sitting behind bars right now, too. He for sure wouldn't be busting broncs.

He was halfway to Wichita Falls, Texas, and he was still second-guessing his decision to compete in this weekend's rodeo. He'd have to ask someone at the rodeo to watch Alex while he rode.

Like who?

He cursed the voice inside his head. If he'd been

more social the past few years, he might have made a friend or two on the circuit, but he'd been a loner for so long that no one had much to say to him. As for asking a buckle bunny to babysit—no way. They'd want something in return for watching Alex, and he couldn't imagine being with another woman any time soon—not after sleeping with Tanya. The cute little barrel racer had left her mark on him—not that she'd ever be happy to see him again after the way he'd ditched her at the motel.

Three and a half hours later, Vic heard rustling noises from the backseat. He checked over his shoulder and caught Alex gripping the crotch of his pants. "You need to use the bathroom?"

The boy nodded.

"Hold on. There's a town five miles up the road." Vic hit the gas. A minute later they passed a sign for Arrow Creek. He took the exit and turned into Letty's Griddle Café. He swung into a parking space, shifted into park, then grabbed Alex from the booster seat—the kid had a death grip on his crotch and wouldn't let go. Vic carried him like a football into the restaurant, his eyes scanning the area for a sign leading to the restrooms.

A waitress with a bleached-blond beehive hairdo glanced up from behind the lunch counter. She took one look at Vic and Alex and pointed to her left. Vic zigzagged between the tables and raced down the short hallway. As soon as he set Alex on his feet in the stall, he pulled down his pants and plopped him on the toilet seat.

"Whew, that was close," Vic said, leaning against the side of the stall. Alex tugged on Vic's jeans. "Finished?"

Alex nodded. Vic helped him straighten his clothes and wash his hands. "It's early for dinner, but we might as well eat while we're here."

They returned to the dining area. When Vic scanned the sea of tables searching for an empty booth, his gaze clashed with Tanya's. She sat in the booth next to the front door. He hadn't noticed her when he entered the café. She must have parked her truck and horse trailer behind the building.

Vic wasn't ready for this meeting—mostly because he hadn't figured out what to say that would excuse him for taking off without telling Tanya why. "This way, Alex." He stopped next to her booth. "Can we join you?"

She didn't take her eyes off Alex. "Sure."

He lifted the boy onto the seat, then slid in behind him, keeping Alex on his right so he wouldn't have to see Vic's scar when he looked at his uncle. If Tanya was surprised to see him with a kid in tow, she hid it well. But her stony expression didn't bode well for him.

"This is Alex," he said. "Alex, this is my…friend, Tanya." Alex drew imaginary circles on the tabletop and wouldn't make eye contact with Tanya.

"You never told me you had a son."

"Alex is my nephew." Relief flashed in Tanya's eyes, followed by a million questions. "I owe you an explanation," he said.

"You don't owe me anything."

She was pissed and he didn't blame her. "I'd like to explain." He glanced at Alex. "When we're alone."

She remained silent, suggesting that he'd have to work his tail off to get that alone time with her.

"We're headed to Wichita Falls. What about you?" he asked.

"Same," she said. "Slingshot took second place in Moriarty and I won enough money to pay for another entry fee."

"Congratulations. Sounds like the horse is coming around." The waitress with the tall hair saved Vic from having to keep the conversation going.

"Howdy, folks. Name's Sally." She placed menus in front of them. "Aren't you a handsome young man?" Sally's gaze swung to Tanya. "How old is your son?"

"Alex is four." Vic cleared his throat. "He's my nephew."

Sally nodded, her eyes skipping over Vic's face—as everyone did.

Except Tanya.

"I'll fetch glasses of water and a milk for your nephew while you look at the menu."

After the waitress walked off, Vic spoke to Alex. "You had chicken for lunch. You want a hamburger?" The boy acted as if he hadn't heard Vic speak. "Or we could order breakfast for supper? Do you like pancakes?" No answer. Vic looked at Tanya, her attention riveted on Alex.

"I got a call from Albuquerque the morning after we..." He couldn't go into detail with his nephew sitting next to him. "Alex is going to be hanging out with me for a while."

Sally returned with their drinks and Vic ordered pancakes and bacon for both him and Alex. Tanya ordered a chicken salad sandwich and a diet cola.

After Sally left, Tanya tried to engage Alex. "Do you like horses, Alex?"

His nephew's finger froze for a second against the tabletop as if considering Tanya's question, then moved in circles again.

"I don't think Alex has ever been around horses or rodeo," Vic said.

"You don't know for sure?"

Vic put his arm around Alex's shoulder and the boy stiffened. "This is the first time we've met, right, buddy?" He winced at Tanya's bug-eyed stare.

"Alex's mother is my younger sister." Vic racked his brain for how much he could tell Tanya without causing more questions.

"How old are you, Alex?" she asked.

"He's four. He'll turn five in September." Hopefully by then Alex would be in a home and his foster parents would give him a proper birthday party.

"What happened to his—"

Vic shook his head, cutting Tanya off. There was no time to explain, because Sally headed their way with their food.

Chapter Five

"What do you mean the first time you've met your nephew?" Tanya whispered after Sally had coaxed Alex to sit at the breakfast counter and watch her make his ice-cream sundae. Vic abandoning her the morning after to run to his nephew's aid sounded a little far-fetched.

"It's a long story," Vic said.

A snarky comment almost slipped from her mouth. Vic deserved her ire for ducking out on her, but he looked so miserable that she didn't have the heart to lash out at him. "I'm a good listener."

"I owe you an apology."

Surprised, she said, "Yes, you do."

"I'm sorry for taking off like I did without waking you first."

"You should have told me you had a family emergency. I would have understood."

"But then I would have had to explain and I…" He rested his elbows on the table and rubbed his head.

"Is it that bad?"

"It's not good."

She didn't care for the twenty-question game they were playing. "Did something happen to Alex's mother?"

Vic's gaze swung to his nephew. "No. My sister's in prison."

Prison? "I'm sorry." She clasped his hand and was surprised when he squeezed back. "Talk to me."

Vic's eyes pleaded with her. Did he yearn to tell her or did he not want to discuss it? Too late for answers— Alex returned to the booth with his sundae.

"This kiddo prefers chocolate ice cream over vanilla. Doesn't like the cherries but loves nuts and whipped cream." Sally winked at Alex, then escaped to take another couple's order.

"Where's home for you?" Tanya knew he was from Albuquerque but didn't know if he lived there or somewhere else when he wasn't riding the circuit.

"The road."

"Are you still planning to rodeo now that you have…" Her eyes flicked to Alex.

"Yes."

He was dead serious.

"Where are you staying for the Wichita rodeo?" he asked.

"I'm boarding Slingshot in Vernon for a couple of days until I compete."

"What do you do when you're not barrel racing?"

"Catch up on laundry. Make phone calls. Surf the web on my laptop." She checked her phone for the time. "The manager at Windy Acres said I could use the cot in his barn." It wasn't the greatest setup, but she didn't have to pay for a motel room and she could keep a close eye on Slingshot—a win-win in her opinion. "What are your plans after Wichita Falls?" Surely he wasn't going to keep the same frantic pace now that he had to care for his nephew.

"Bakersfield, California, then Texas and Nevada." He must have read the question in her eyes, because he said, "Alex doesn't turn five until the end of September, so he can't enroll in kindergarten for another year."

"He's awfully young to drag around the country with you." As soon as the words left her mouth, she knew she'd overstepped her bounds. Vic clenched his jaw, and the scar across his cheek turned white.

"I've had my schedule planned out since last year. As long as I keep riding well, I'll be in Vegas this December. This might be my last shot at a title." He stared at Alex. "Besides, CYFD is hoping to place him in a home before the end of summer."

Tanya understood Vic's urgency. He wasn't getting any younger and he had another good year, maybe two, left in the sport. But Alex was family, and the little boy, not Vic's rodeo schedule, should be a priority.

"We'll be fine, won't we, buddy?" Vic ruffled Alex's hair, but the boy barely acknowledged his uncle's affectionate touch. Tanya got the sense that there was a lot more involved with Alex's situation than Vic having temporary custody of him.

Her heart broke for the little guy. She wanted to ask what had happened to the person who'd been caring for Alex while his mother was in prison, but now wasn't the time.

"Where are you competing after Wichita Falls?" Vic asked.

"I'm not sure." If she didn't win any money in the rodeo, she'd seriously have to consider returning to Colorado. Going into debt just because she wanted one last season before she put barrel racing behind her wasn't smart. She just needed a little more time to wrap her head around leaving the sport. At least when she walked away from rodeo for good, she'd go back to a job she loved—training her stepfather's Appaloosas.

"Tanya, I'm really sorry about—"

She waved off his apology. "No worries." She couldn't hold a grudge against Vic when Alex was the reason he'd left. She was relieved that he hadn't taken off because he regretted sleeping with her.

A stilted silence hovered between them, and Tanya's gaze swung to the boy. It wasn't just her and Vic anymore, trying to cross paths with their rodeo schedules. "I better go. I want to arrive in Vernon before dark." She dropped a ten-dollar bill on the table and slid from the booth. "Alex, it was nice meeting you." She smiled. "Have fun at the rodeos with your uncle." She purposefully avoided eye contact with Vic and walked out of the diner.

"LADIES AND GENTLEMEN, it's time for the saddle-bronc competition."

Vic crouched in front of Alex and looked him in the eye. "I need to you to sit there and not move until I come back for you." He pointed to the folding chair behind him in the cowboy ready area. A few minutes earlier he'd gotten up the courage to approach two buckle bunnies ogling the cowboys. He'd planned to ask if Alex could sit with them while he rode, but as soon as he made eye contact the women turned and hurried away.

As a last resort he'd given twenty dollars to an old man named Roy who watched the gear bags for the cowboys. Roy promised to make sure Alex sat in the chair until Vic returned.

"I'll be back after my ride." He walked Alex to the chair and lifted him onto the seat. "If you wait here and don't move, I'll buy you a treat before we leave today. Okay?"

Alex looked at him but didn't speak. Last night Vic had lain in bed and stared at the ceiling wondering how he was going to find a therapist for Alex when he didn't stay in one place more than twenty-four hours.

"Hey, Vicario! You better hurry or you'll scratch!"

"Don't move." Vic hustled to the chute and climbed the rails, then straddled the bronc. For a split second he'd forgotten the horse's name. *Duster.* Worrying about Alex was messing with his concentration. He threaded the rope through his fingers and tried to push everything but him and the horse out of his mind.

"Let's see if Duster can live up to his namesake and toss Vicario in the dust," the announcer said as the fans stomped their feet. "Don't count on it, folks. This cowboy puts up a good fight. Vicario is looking to fill a spot at the National Finals Rodeo in December and he needs a win this afternoon."

Vic nodded to the gateman. Duster sprang from the chute and attempted to dislodge him with a vicious buck but didn't succeed. Vic counted the seconds in his head and eased up on his grip when he reached eight—only the buzzer didn't sound until a second later. By then Vic had already slipped in the saddle and the mistake would cost him first place. He dove for the ground, then rolled to his feet and jogged back to the chute.

His gaze swung to the folding chair in the corner. Empty. His heart dropped to his stomach. He glanced at the stall Roy had been sitting in front of, and the old man was gone, too. Panic held him immobile. He grabbed the shirtsleeve of a passing cowboy. "Have you seen a little boy wandering around here?"

The man yanked his arm free and scowled. "No."

Vic hurried through the cowboy ready area, keeping his eyes peeled for Roy or Alex. He found them outside by the calf corral. "Alex!" Vic shouted. He joined the pair, his heart slowly inching back into his chest.

"I told you to stay in the chair, Alex."

"Just showin' the kid the cows," Roy said.

Angry that he'd had the crap scared out of him, Vic grabbed Alex's hand. "C'mon." They returned to the chute area to retrieve his gear bag and then Vic pulled Alex aside and squatted in front of him. "You have to do what I say or this isn't going to work. When I tell you to stay—" he sounded as if he were talking to a dog "—you can't wander off no matter who says it's okay. Do you understand?" He didn't want to scare the boy with stranger-danger stories, but damn it, he needed Alex to realize his safety was serious business. "I was worried when I couldn't find you," he said. "I thought something bad might have happened to you." He ruffled the mop of black hair in need of a cut. "Don't do that again. Okay?"

Alex nodded, reassuring Vic that he got the warning. "I bet you're hungry." They walked to the concession stand, where Vic ordered corn dogs and lemonades. He didn't know a thing about raising kids, but if Maria didn't allow her twin sons to drink soda, he figured it was best to keep Alex off the stuff, too.

They found an out-of-the-way spot to sit and watch the rest of the rodeo. Normally Vic would be on the road to the next town, but today's scare had forced him to reevaluate his goals. The thought of quitting rodeo—walking away from twelve years of hard work without a title to show for his efforts—didn't hurt half as bad as not being able to present Cruz with a national-championship buckle. Vic had dedicated his life to winning a buckle for his friend, and coming up short made him feel hollow inside and spitfire angry.

He blamed the anger on his mother. Hate was a strong word, but that was the first one that came to mind when he thought of her. How could one woman destroy so many lives? His mother had used drugs on and off most of Vic's life, and it had never been pretty when she came down from her high.

He stared at the top of Alex's head. Had Vic's mother mistreated him while he was in her care? It wasn't enough that she'd physically injured Vic when he'd been younger, but his mother left everyone she came in contact with emotionally scarred. And now her actions were robbing Vic of the only way he knew how to make amends for a past wrong.

The anger burned a hole in his gut. If he walked away from busting broncs, his mother would have won again. He couldn't let that happen. He had to find a way to continue riding and keep Alex safe until Renee placed him in a foster home. Vic was almost desperate enough to call Maria and ask if she'd take care of Alex. He knew she would, but then he'd have to tell her the reason he was picking rodeo over his nephew and he didn't want Cruz to know he was chasing a title for him.

"Ladies and gentlemen, it's time for the women's barrel-racing event."

Vic's thoughts turned to Tanya. So much had happened he'd barely had time to think about the night he'd spent with her at the Sweet Dreams Inn. If he closed his eyes, he could still feel her softness, smell her sweetness. After the first round of lovemaking, he'd tried to pull away, but Tanya had slid her leg between his thighs and rested her head on his chest, then had fallen asleep seconds later. At first her weight had felt suffocating, but when he'd wrapped his arms around her and run his fingers over her back, counting the bumps in her spine, a sense of rightness and peace had filled him. With her warmth surrounding him, he'd closed his eyes and drifted off to sleep.

"First up is Tanya McGee from Longmont, Colorado. Tanya's riding Slingshot, a horse with a reputation for being contrary." The rodeo fans next to Vic and Alex chuckled. "Let's see if Tanya can get Slingshot to cooperate."

"Look over there." Vic pointed to the alley where Tanya and the horse would enter from. Alex watched the opening, and a few seconds later Tanya and Sling-shot ran into the arena, heading for the first barrel. Alex scooted to the edge of his seat, the corn dog in his hand forgotten.

Tanya and Slingshot made the first turn, then sprinted for the second barrel. Vic held his breath, hoping the horse wouldn't balk—he didn't. They cleared the second barrel, and just when Vic believed the pair might finally turn in a winning time, Slingshot took the third barrel too wide and lost valuable seconds. Tanya tried to make up for the error on the sprint home, but Slingshot didn't give it his all.

The announcer made a sound of sympathy. "Tanya and Slingshot came in at a little over eighteen seconds. Better luck next time, cowgirl."

Vic glanced at Alex. "She didn't win," he said. Alex kept staring at the alley as if waiting for Tanya to come out again. "Let's go tell her we're sorry she lost."

Vic lifted Alex into his arms and carried him out of the stands, then set him down and took his hand. They went outside by the livestock pens and found Tanya walking Slingshot. Vic stopped a safe distance away. "Slingshot looked better tonight."

Tanya's sober expression insisted the opposite. Her gaze softened when she spoke to his nephew. "Did you enjoy the rodeo?"

Alex nodded.

"A couple more competitions and Slingshot might go all the way for you," he said.

"That's not going to happen."

"What do you mean?" he asked.

"We're done. This was our last rodeo." She walked Slingshot into the corral, removed his saddle and reins, then set the tack over the rail and closed the gate behind her.

Vic took Alex's hand and walked closer. "Why is this your last rodeo?"

Her gaze focused on the pickups parked across the lot and her lips pressed into a thin line.

"What's wrong?" Vic touched her arm and she looked at him, eyes shimmering with tears.

"I'm broke." She shrugged off his touch. "I can't afford anymore entry fees, much less gas to drive to the next rodeo."

If it was about money... "I can float you a loan until you start winning." Shoot, it was the least he could do after ditching her at the motel.

"I can't take your money." That Vic had offered to help warmed Tanya's heart. There wasn't a whole lot of support for her back at Red Rock. If she asked Mason for a little more time to prove Slingshot's worth, he'd say no and tell her to pack it up and come home. "It's not only the entry fees. I've got ten bucks left in my checking account. I don't have enough money to feed Slingshot, much less pay for motel rooms or boarding him between competitions." She laughed, the sound humorless. "And unless I take first place in every event from here on out, I'd never win enough money to repay you."

"I have an idea." Vic's gaze swung between her and Alex.

A sixth sense told Tanya she wasn't going to like his plan.

"What if we travel the circuit together?"

She shook his head. "That wouldn't be a good idea."

"I'm not insinuating that we…you know…" He lowered his voice. "…be together that way."

Tanya wasn't sure if she should be insulted or not. Maybe Vic hadn't enjoyed their lovemaking as much as he'd led her to believe. "What's the catch?" she asked, then immediately wished she hadn't.

"If we travel together…" He dropped his gaze to Alex and suddenly she understood why he was eager to pay her rodeo expenses.

"You need a babysitter," she said.

"Not really a babysitter as much as someone to keep an eye on Alex when I'm riding."

Alex's sad brown eyes tugged at Tanya's heartstrings. Being around the sweet little boy wouldn't be a hardship, but it hurt her pride that Vic was offering her money to play nanny to his nephew.

"Thanks, but I'll pass."

"Why?"

Couldn't he see that he'd offended her? What former lover appreciated being needed as a nanny?

Use him back. Take his money and keep working with Slingshot. You know the horse is just one rodeo away from winning. "How am I supposed to keep an eye on Alex when I'm working with Slingshot between rodeos?" Never mind the fact that they wouldn't always compete in the same rodeos.

"I'll be around between rodeos and I can watch Alex while you're working with the horse."

"I don't enter as many rodeos as you do. And it's not

fair to make my horse travel in the trailer for long periods of time. That's why I board him between rodeos."

"We'll find places to keep him along the way. It won't be that difficult. I promise."

Tanya studied Alex. She'd never been around kids before. And it was obvious that Vic's nephew needed special help to cope with whatever had happened to him. What if she said or did something that made things worse for the boy? She glanced at Vic, and the pleading look in his eyes set her back on her heels. It would be so easy to cave in to him. He'd made her feel things she'd never felt before—not even with Beau.

"Please, Tanya," Vic whispered. "I'll pay all your expenses…food, lodging, clothes, feed, boarding."

That was more than generous, but she wished Vic wanted her with him for himself and not for his nephew.

"You have unfinished business with Slingshot. Here's your chance to see it through to the end," he said.

The thought of going home and having to admit that her pride had gotten in the way of her good judgment didn't sit well with Tanya. Vic was giving her one more chance to prove her instincts about Slingshot were correct. The horse was a winner. And Vic was allowing her the chance to give barrel racing a proper goodbye.

When a loud bang rent the air, Alex flung himself against Tanya and buried his face between her legs. Automatically she dropped to her knees and wrapped her arms around his shaking body. "It's okay, honey." She caught the sad expression on Vic's face as he watched his nephew cling to her. The bronc rider needed her as much as Alex did—he just didn't know it.

"I suppose we'll be following your rodeo schedule?" She knew the answer before she'd asked the question.

"If I have a long enough break between events, you're more than welcome to take off and compete. Just so we meet up again when it's time for my next ride."

For a short while Tanya had believed Vic was different than all the rest of the rodeo cowboys. But in the end he was pretty much the same—rodeo came first. Everything else came second. Her eyes were wide-open going into this arrangement, and that was all it was— an arrangement.

"How long do you need me for?" she asked.

"Until they find Alex a good foster home."

That could be days, weeks or months. Her arms tightened around the little boy. "Okay."

"Okay…you'll travel with us?"

She nodded. "Where to next?"

"Bakersfield, California."

Tanya was familiar with the Kern County Sheriff Reserve Stampede Days Rodeo. "That's not a large event."

"I'm competing as a favor to a friend."

"It's probably too late for me to enter that one," she said.

"I'm headed to Bridgeport, Texas, after Bakersfield."

A PRCA-sanctioned rodeo. She'd give Slingshot a rest while Vic competed at the Stampede Days Rodeo, and then she'd ride in Bridgeport. "I have to buy feed before we leave."

He removed his wallet and handed her a credit card. "Get whatever you need." Vic reached for Alex's hand, but the boy wouldn't release Tanya's leg.

"You want to tag along with me while I buy food for Slingshot?" She offered Alex her hand and when he squeezed her fingers tightly, Tanya knew she'd made the right decision.

As they walked away from Vic, she decided it was a good thing Alex wouldn't be around more than a few weeks, because she was already infatuated with his uncle and the last thing she needed was to have her heart broken by a miniature cowboy, too.

Chapter Six

"Thank you again for letting me board Slingshot until after the rodeo tomorrow." Tanya smiled at Glenda Krammer. The woman and her husband, Fred, had become friends with her stepfather after meeting at an Appaloosa horse auction a few years ago.

"I'll let you in on a secret," Glenda said. "Your father informed me that you might drop by."

Tanya laughed. Mason had probably phoned every acquaintance across the country warning them to be on the lookout for her. Glenda wasn't charging her to board Slingshot at their farm north of Bakersfield. Tanya suspected Mason had already paid the bill. At least Vic wouldn't have to cough up his own cash this time.

Glenda nodded to Alex swinging on the tire hanging from the tree next to the house. "Mason didn't mention anything about a little boy and a handsome cowboy traveling with you."

"It's a long story that would only worry my father or mother if they found out."

"I won't say a word." Glenda pressed a finger against her lips.

"You promise?" Tanya was dying to talk about the situation with someone.

Glenda drew an X on her chest. "Cross my heart."

"I met Victor at a rodeo. We became…friends." Friendship was a safer word than lovers—just in case Glenda spilled the beans. "Then Vic got a call and took off for Albuquerque and the next time I ran into him, he was with Alex."

"He didn't tell you he had a son?"

"Alex is Vic's nephew. The boy's grandmother disappeared and his mother is in prison, so Vic has temporary custody of Alex until they can place him in a foster home."

"Wow. That sounds like the makings of a movie. The boy doesn't have a father?"

"Vic never said what happened to Alex's father."

"How did you end up traveling together?" Glenda's gaze remained on Alex and she smiled when the boy jumped off the tire swing midair and then raced back to do it all over again.

"Vic and I made a bargain. We'd travel to his rodeos and I'd watch Alex while he competed, and in return for my help, he's paying my entry fees when I compete and my travel expenses until Alex returns to Albuquerque."

"So you're a nanny and a barrel racer."

Tanya snagged Glenda's arm. "You can't tell Mason that I'm almost flat broke. He'll put up a big stink."

"He's convinced Slingshot is unpredictable and needs to be sold."

"The horse has heart. I'm not ready to give up on him. He just needs more time on the circuit."

"Mason and your mother are worried about you. They don't want to see you get hurt."

"I know." Tanya sympathized with her parents' concern. It was common knowledge she'd busted her leg pretty badly in the car accident and the doctors had used plates and screws to repair the damage to her tibia and fibula. But what most people didn't know was that she'd caught pneumonia while recovering in the hospital and had almost died fighting the infection. After she'd left the hospital, Mason and her mother had hovered over her for months, wanting to rush her to the doctor after every sneeze or cough. Not until Tanya had finished physical therapy and proven she could walk fine and breathe fine did her folks ease up.

She hadn't expected them to support her decision to return to the circuit, but barrel racing was such an important part of her life and she wouldn't be at peace until she gave the sport a proper send-off.

Glenda waved at the pickup approaching the yard. Fred parked in front of the house and joined them at the corral. "I think I know why Slingshot gets flustered in the arena," he said.

"I'm all ears." Tanya had told the couple about the horse's struggles.

"Instead of pressing your thigh against his side when you head into the turn, release the pressure and see what he does."

"Give him free rein to take the barrel at whatever speed he wants?" That sounded dangerous.

"You might be trying too hard to guide him around the barrel. He knows what to do."

Mason had taught Tanya the ins and outs of training a barrel-racing horse, and riders used their thighs to control the animal's momentum. For most horses that worked fine, but Slingshot had a mind of his own. Maybe she was fighting him too hard. "Okay. Let's give it a try and see what he does."

"I'll put out the barrels. You saddle up Slingshot." Fred walked off, calling to a ranch hand as he entered the training barn.

"Will you keep an eye on Alex for me?" Tanya asked Glenda.

"We'll come watch." Glenda went to get Alex.

Tanya entered the corral and spoke to Slingshot. "Hey, big guy. Guess what? Fred thinks you should be the boss when we race, and we're going to see if he's right."

Twenty minutes later, the barrels were in place. Tanya and Slingshot waited outside the barn ready to race inside when the signal was given. When Fred appeared in the doorway and waved, Tanya leaned forward, then tapped her boot heels against Slingshot. The horse responded and raced into the barn. She guided him toward the right barrel first using the reins to signal the direction but resisted the urge to squeeze his flanks with her thighs.

As they approached the turn, Slingshot didn't check his speed. Then a second later he put on the brakes and Tanya almost flew over his head. Confused, Slingshot stamped his feet.

"He was waiting for you to signal him to slow down, and when you didn't, he panicked." Fred waved her out of the barn. "Give it another try."

Tanya and Slingshot returned outside, and when Fred signaled again they raced into the barn. This time Slingshot didn't stop. He took the barrel at full speed and caught Tanya off balance. After he cleared the barrel she pulled back on the reins and he trotted to a stop.

"What happened?" Fred asked.

"Nothing." She laughed. "I was about to fall off. You got any advice on how I can keep my seat?"

"You're going to have to rely on your stomach muscles to stay in the saddle. And remember when he makes the turn you can use your thighs for balance. It's just the approach that you don't want your legs pressing into him."

Tanya and Slingshot worked for an hour until she was certain that he understood she wouldn't slow him down on the approach. "I think this guy needs a rest," she said, climbing down from the saddle.

"You'd better call me when you run him next and tell me how he does." Fred took his reins. "I'll have one of the hands give him a rubdown."

"I'm sure he'd appreciate that." She patted Slingshot's neck. "I'm eager to see how he responds in competition now."

"You be careful. He's a powerful horse. If he really lets loose you could get hurt."

After Fred and Slingshot left the barn, Tanya joined Glenda and Alex. "What did you think of Slingshot?" She ruffled the boy's hair. "Do we have a chance of winning?"

Alex looked up at Tanya, then ducked his head. He was such a cute kid and her heart hurt for him. He must feel so alone. She knew how she'd felt when her father died. At ten years old she'd been a tomboy and had been closer to her father than her mother. She'd lost her best friend when he'd passed away.

A horn honked and Tanya glanced toward the barn doors. Vic parked his pickup next to Fred's. "Your uncle is back, Alex."

"Are you three eating with us tonight?" Glenda asked.

Tanya appreciated the invitation, but she needed a break from Glenda's chatter. She could talk the ear off a donkey. "I think we're heading into town for dinner."

"Okay, then. Have fun."

After Glenda left the barn, Tanya took Alex's hand and met Vic in the driveway. "How do you feel about eating supper in town?"

"Sure," Vic said. "Maybe Alex would like to go with me to the barbershop for a haircut."

She ruffled Alex's dark locks. "You want to cut this pretty hair?"

Vic studied his nephew. "Have you ever been to the barber?"

Alex didn't answer his uncle.

Tanya smiled at the boy. "Staying handsome is hard work. Ask your uncle. He knows." She grasped Alex's hand and crossed the driveway, Vic's gaze following her the whole way.

"Who's first?" The barbershop owner glanced between Alex and Vic.

"I'll go." Vic climbed into the barber chair and sat.

An older man with a name tag that said Mel threw a cape over Vic and sprayed his hair with water.

"What'll it be?" he asked.

"Just a trim." Vic didn't need a haircut, but he was determined that his nephew got one. Tanya thought Alex's long locks were cute, but Vic worried the boy might be teased by other kids. Alex would have a difficult enough time adjusting to a new family. He didn't need to fend off bullies because his hair was too long. Besides, Vic didn't want others saying he wasn't taking proper care of his nephew.

Mel flipped the pair of scissors between his fingers with expertise and Vic watched Tanya and Alex in the mirror across from him. After he'd dropped Tanya and Slingshot off at the Krammers' ranch, he couldn't get away fast enough. Traveling in close quarters with her had him questioning his sanity. Tanya was a huge distraction, and all he could think about was getting her alone so he could kiss her. He'd driven into Bakersfield earlier and filled his gas tank, then scoped out the parking at the arena before making himself comfortable in a coffee shop, where he checked out the PRCA rodeo standings on his iPhone and searched for children's therapists in the area.

He'd found Dr. Melissa Harper, and her office happened to be located down the block from the barbershop. He spoke to a receptionist named Ann and explained Alex's situation. Ann had agreed to call Alex's social worker and get more information while he waited in the coffee shop. A half hour later Ann informed him that Dr. Harper was willing to see Alex and conduct

an initial evaluation after office hours at seven tonight.
He hoped having Tanya along would ease Alex's anxiety at being interviewed by the therapist. And he was
pretty sure Dr. Harper would notice that Alex hardly
ever made eye contact with Vic. It was obvious the boy
didn't trust his uncle.

*Maybe he doesn't want to get close to you because
he's afraid you'll abandon him like his mother and
grandmother.* The thought punched Vic in the gut, because in the end that was exactly what he would do—
return Alex to Albuquerque to live with someone else.

Vic and his siblings hadn't had a fairy-tale childhood, but he hoped Alex was placed with a nice couple. The tyke deserved to be loved and cared for and he
needed the security of knowing he was safe.

"How's that?" The barber stared at Vic in the mirror.

"Good. Thanks." He waited for the barber to remove
the cape, then got up from the chair. "Your turn, Alex."

His nephew leaned against Tanya. The kid was nervous. Vic crouched in front of him. "What if you sit on
my lap while you get your hair trimmed?" Vic had no
idea what made him say that, but Tanya's smile insisted
he'd done the right thing.

"Great idea, Alex." When the boy didn't budge,
Tanya said, "And I'll be right here. I'm not going anywhere."

Vic held out his hand and Alex placed his small fist
in his palm. The tightness in Vic's chest unraveled and
he breathed a sigh of relief. Vic sat down in the chair
and lifted Alex onto his lap.

The barber draped the cape over them, momentarily

covering Alex's face. "Tanya, where's Alex? I can't see him."

"Did he leave the barbershop?" Tanya laughed when Alex pulled the cape down and his head popped free.

"Here he is!" Vic said.

Alex made eye contact with him in the mirror, and Vic silently cheered. In that moment he realized how much he'd wanted to connect with the boy. Vic had been a crappy uncle before tragic circumstances had brought him and Alex together. They wouldn't have a lot of time together, but he hoped he could use it to make up for some of the pain and disappointment the kid had experienced so far in his life.

While the barber trimmed Alex's hair, Vic's gaze clashed with Tanya's in the mirror. They still hadn't talked about their night at the motel three weeks ago. Did she want more than that one night with him?

"What do you think?" Mel asked.

Vic stared at Alex. "Is it short enough?"

Alex leaned around Vic and when Tanya gave him the thumbs-up sign, Alex ducked beneath the cape and slid off Vic's lap.

"I guess it's short enough." Vic waited at the register until Mel swept up the hair, then went behind the counter and took Vic's credit card. He gave Mel a five-dollar tip for the haircuts, then they left the shop and walked down the block where Vic had parked his pickup. As they drew nearer he caught Alex ogling the mechanical-pony ride outside the entrance of drugstore.

Vic stopped next to the ride and fished two quarters from his pocket. "Hop on, Alex."

The boy straddled the horse and Vic dropped the quarters into the slot. The pony jolted forward before settling into an easy rocking rhythm.

"Did you ride these as a kid?" Tanya asked.

"A few times." Vic hadn't really ridden them, but he and the group of teenagers he'd hung around had broken into the coin boxes and stolen the money.

"Before my father died he'd take me to town every Sunday and let me ride the pony in front of the grocery store while he went inside and bought a newspaper," Tanya said.

He wanted to ask about Tanya's father and her childhood, but what was the use when they'd go their separate ways once Alex returned to Albuquerque? The night in the motel was nothing more than that—one night. The only reason they were together now was because of Alex.

So take advantage of the situation.

The temptation to pick up where they'd left off at the Sweet Dreams Inn was strong. Why couldn't they have a bit of fun while they took care of his nephew? Then they'd go their separate ways. No fuss. No mess. No broken hearts.

Do you really believe what you feel for Tanya is pure lust and nothing more?

Vic hated the stupid voice in his head. If he slept with Tanya again, *feelings* would be involved. He already admired her spunk and determination, and when she smiled at Alex, the softness in her eyes tugged at his heartstrings. He appreciated her kindness toward his nephew and he had no idea what he would have done if she hadn't agreed to help him watch Alex during the height of his rodeo season.

"You look like a real cowboy." Tanya took a picture of Alex with her phone.

Vic checked his watch. They had two hours to kill before Alex's appointment with the therapist. "Speaking of real cowboys, Alex needs a hat and boots." Something to remember his uncle by.

"Great idea." They hopped into the pickup and asked Siri for the location of the nearest Western-wear store. Ten minutes later Vic pulled into the parking lot. When they entered the business, a young man showed them to the children's boot aisle. Alex sat in a chair while the salesman searched for styles in his size. After trying on three different pairs, Alex pointed to the brown boots.

Tanya nudged Vic and then dropped her gaze to his boots. Alex had chosen boots similar to Vic's. His hearted thumped heavily in his chest. He might feel as though he and Alex were struggling to communicate, but Vic must be doing something right if his nephew wanted to copy him.

"Now we need a hat," Vic said.

The salesman had Alex try on different ones, but again the boy picked a hat like Vic's. When they left the store, Vic spoke to Tanya. "I bet there's a Dave and Buster's close by."

Tanya's expression lit up. "Pizza sounds good and Alex will like the games."

Alex didn't comment. He was too preoccupied with his new boots.

"Pizza it is." A short ride later Vic pulled up to the

restaurant and entertainment chain. "I'll get us a table and order the pizza while you two check out the games," Tanya said.

Alex stared wide-eyed, frozen in place. This was probably too much for him to take in all at once. Vic walked him over to a motorcycle simulator. "Hop on." Once Alex sat on the small bike seat, Vic swiped the card he'd purchased and the bike moved back and forth in front of a screen that flashed images of busy city streets.

While Alex enjoyed the ride, Vic's gaze searched for Tanya and found her waiting at a table in the dining room. He waved at her to join them, but she shook her head. "We have time for one more ride before we eat. How about you and I try the Typhoon?" They sat side by side in front of another large screen. Vic swiped his card and suddenly they were in a roller coaster. Their seats jiggled and shook as if the ride were real. Alex's eyes grew huge and he reached for Vic's hand.

"You okay, buddy?"

Alex smiled—a happy smile—when his chair rocked sideways.

The ride lasted for a full minute; then the coaster in the video slowed down and their seats stopped moving. "That made me hungry. Let's see if the pizza is ready."

"You two look like you had fun," Tanya said.

"Alex liked the Typhoon," he said. "You should try it."

"Not after eating, thanks." The waiter delivered their pizza and Alex gobbled his food in record time—a big change from when the kid had picked at his pancakes the first time they ate a meal with Tanya. After he finished his slice, Vic said, "You've been eyeing that claw machine." The glass cabinet, standing a few yards away, was filled with neon-colored stuffed animals. "Go ahead and take a look."

Alex slipped out of his chair and went over to the machine. Vic turned his seat so he could keep an eye on his nephew.

"You're really patient with him," Tanya said. "If I didn't know better, I'd assume you were a father."

"I'm winging it, but I appreciate the vote of confidence." He cleared his throat. "I made an appointment with a therapist for Alex here in town. She's willing to see him at seven."

"Tonight?"

He nodded. "I don't know how he'll react, but he's comfortable around you and I was hoping…"

"I'll help in any way I can."

"Thanks."

"Tell me about your family," she said.

Vic hated airing his family's dirty laundry. He'd rather no one on the circuit learn about his past. But Tanya deserved to know the truth, since she was a big part of the reason he was able to stick to his rodeo schedule.

"My family's pretty dysfunctional," he said, never taking his eyes off Alex. "My dad left years ago. I don't remember much about him."

"I'm sorry."

If Tanya was saying I'm sorry now, what would she say when she heard the rest of his sordid tale? "My older brother was shot and killed by police during an armed robbery. My eldest sister got pregnant by a gangbanger and ended up committing suicide after she found out she was pregnant."

Vic had no idea if Maria Fitzgerald had told Cruz what had happened to Camila. His sister had been the reason Vic had borrowed a gun from a friend and had gone to confront the gang leader and demand he do right by Camila. Cruz had tagged along for support, and when Vic pulled the gun out of his pants, Cruz had made a grab for it. The weapon discharged, wounding the gang leader in the shoulder. A few minutes later Cruz was sitting in the backseat of a police car, his rodeo career over.

Tanya squeezed his hand. "So it's just you, your mother and Natalia now?"

"Yeah. I stuck around for a while after Camila died then I left home and started rodeoing." Vic kept his gaze averted. He didn't want to see sympathy in Tanya's eyes. Bad stuff had happened in Vic's family, but other kids in the barrio had suffered, too—some even more. Most of his friends had lost a sibling or relative to gang shootings, drug overdoses or violent crime.

"I was wondering about Alex's mom."

"She's in prison for prostitution and my mother's been a drug addict since my father left her." He sucked in a deep breath. "I think my mother may have gone out to buy drugs and gotten high the night she left Alex home alone."

"She never came back?"

"The police haven't found her yet."

Tanya sucked in a quick breath. "I hope nothing bad happened to her."

Vic didn't care what happened to her. He stopped caring after what she'd done to him. He caught Tanya staring at his face.

"How did you get that scar?" she asked.

"My mother cut me when I was sixteen."

She gasped. "My God, what happened, Vic?"

"Camila slept with my mother's boyfriend." Vic's sister had been flirting with the guy for weeks and Vic had warned her to knock it off. "My mother walked in on them. The boyfriend escaped the apartment, but my mother went after Camila with a butcher knife. The yelling woke me up. I tried to talk my mother down, but she was high on drugs." Vic closed his eyes when an image of his mother's angry face flashed through his mind. "I jumped in front of Camila and the knife got me instead of her." His mother had fled the apartment and Vic had taken a ride with the paramedics to the hospital.

"They didn't press charges against your mom?"

His mother hadn't even remembered that night when she returned home two days later. She'd been horrified at what she'd done and had promised to quit the drugs. Both Camila and Natalia had begged him not to let the police prosecute their mother, so he hadn't.

"Do you think your mother harmed Alex while she had custody of him?"

"I don't know." He hoped not.

"I'll see if Alex wants to play the claw machine." Tanya left the table and Vic expelled a harsh breath.

After that gruesome story he'd be lucky if she didn't

wake up tomorrow and announce that she was returning to Colorado instead of heading down the road with him and his nephew.

Chapter Seven

"Ladies and gentlemen, we're about to kick off the saddle-bronc competition here at the Kern County Sheriff Reserve Stampede Days Rodeo in Bakersfield, California!"

Tanya held Alex's hand as they made their way into the stands to watch Vic ride late Saturday afternoon. She and Alex had slept at the Krammers' ranch, but tonight they were staying in town so Dr. Harper could meet with Alex one more time before they headed down the road.

The therapist had spent almost an hour with Alex, and she and Vic had been allowed to observe the session through a two-way mirror. Although Alex hadn't spoken to Dr. Harper, he'd drawn several pictures and had given the therapist an idea of what he was feeling— mostly fear and insecurity. Anyone would have come to that conclusion after the boy's experience. The therapist had asked Vic to bring Alex in for another visit after the rodeo, at which time she'd have a few suggestions prepared to help Alex cope better.

Tanya found a spot in the shade and sat. "If your

uncle makes the second go-round today, you'll have the chance to see him compete twice."

Alex remained quiet, munching on his popcorn. Watching the therapist interview him had been heartbreaking. It was as if he'd shrunk inside himself, hoping to disappear.

"How do you think Slingshot will do today?" She hadn't planned on competing in this rodeo, but when Vic checked in at the scorer's table he'd learned there were still two slots open in the barrel-racing event. He insisted on paying her entry fee and she couldn't refuse. She wanted to find out if the training she'd done with Slingshot at the Krammers' ranch stuck or not.

Because of a traffic accident on Interstate 204, which was holding up three of her competitors, the board of directors switched the order of rodeo events and moved barrel racing to the final competition of the evening.

A pair of clowns entered the arena to entertain the fans, drawing Alex's attention. She snuck a handful of his popcorn and winked at him when he looked at her. Then he offered her the box. "No, thanks, honey. If I eat too much before I compete, I get an upset stomach." Alex's gaze dropped to her stomach and Tanya leaned close and whispered in his ear. "Don't tell anyone, but I get really nervous before I ride Slingshot. I want to win so badly, but I'm always afraid I won't."

She hadn't expected a response, so when he patted her thigh as if trying to reassure her, Tanya couldn't resist hugging him. Even though he didn't talk, he knew more than he let on.

"Your uncle is the last one to compete." Alex was

too young to understand just how good a rodeo athlete Vic was. "Maybe one day you'll grow up to ride broncs, too."

While the announcer went over the rules of the event for the greenhorns, Tanya's gaze zeroed in on the cowboy ready area. Vic stood by himself away from the other cowboys waiting for their names to be called. When she first became aware of him, she'd believed he'd kept to himself because his scar intimidated his competitors. Now she wondered if he'd gone through life solo because he was embarrassed by the tragedies that had struck his family and he wanted to avoid people poking their noses into his personal life.

Tanya's heart ached when she imagined the horrific scene that played out the day Vic's mother had wounded him with a butcher knife. A mother was supposed to protect her children, not harm them. And big brothers shouldn't have to protect little sisters from their mothers, either.

She brushed a lock of hair off Alex's forehead. Aside from the same dark hair and brown eyes, Tanya couldn't see any resemblance between Vic and Alex. "The new haircut looks handsome on you." The corner of his mouth tilted upward just a fraction. Maybe Alex would gift her with a wide smile before they were forced to part ways for good.

Considering nothing but bad memories waited for Vic in Albuquerque, Tanya admired him for racing to his nephew's aide. Her anger at him for leaving her stranded at the motel was a distant memory. Sure, it would have been nice if he'd woken her to explain why he had to leave, but in all honesty she might have done the same thing had she received such disturbing news about her family.

Life was crazy and full of twists and turns. What would the morning after have been like between her and Vic if he hadn't gotten that phone call? Since they'd begun traveling together, Tanya had caught Vic's heated stare when he thought she wasn't paying attention. The attraction was still there between them, simmering right below the surface.

"There's your uncle. Do you see him?" Tanya pointed to the chute across the arena.

Alex sat up straighter. Even though he wasn't openly affectionate toward his uncle, she noticed the boy was becoming more relaxed around Vic.

"We're down to our last two riders of the evening," the announcer said. "Eighty-four is the score to beat. We've saved the best competitors for last, and I'm predicting one of these cowboys will go home a winner."

Tanya applauded and Alex did, too, only he forgot he held the box of popcorn and pieces of the snack flew into the air, landing on their laps. Tanya laughed and Alex almost smiled. By the time they brushed the popcorn from their clothing, the chute gate opened and a cowboy named Russ Terry vaulted into the arena on the back of Demon.

The black gelding spun more than kicked, but the cowboy held on. Tanya was no expert on spurring, but she'd seen enough events to pick out which cowboys were good at it and which ones were mediocre. Russ was good—almost as good as Vic.

The buzzer sounded and the crowd offered a standing ovation. Tanya snickered. The fans would be jumping in the stands after Vic's ride.

"Our final contestant this evening is Victor Vicario from Albuquerque, New Mexico. Vicario's been riding the circuit for over a decade, so this cowboy knows his way around a bronc." The crowd stomped their boots against the metal bleachers. "If Vicario keeps riding like he's been doing these past few months, then you might see him in Vegas this December."

A shrill whistle rent the air, and Tanya snapped her head sideways. A group of buckle bunnies waved posters with Vic's name on them. They all looked like beauty queens—gorgeous figures and pretty faces.

Tanya felt dowdy compared to the women. Beau had said she was cute—not pretty, cute. All Vic had to do was snap his fingers and any one of the lovelies would go off with him.

But he took you *to the motel.*

The thought did little to comfort her. Although the night they'd spent together was always there between them, Vic hadn't attempted to kiss her since he returned from Albuquerque with Alex—and he'd had numerous opportunities.

"Vicario's drawn Torpedo, an explosive bronc known to throw cowboys over his head when he plants his hooves in the dirt. Let's see if Vicario can keep his seat and beat Terry's score of eighty-eight to win first place."

The crowd grew quiet, their attention on the chute, where Vic straddled Torpedo. He took only a few seconds to prepare for his ride. As soon as he'd threaded the reins through his fingers, he nodded to the gate man and the chute opened. Torpedo escaped his confinement with a vicious buck and Tanya winced when she imagined the strain on Vic's spine. Torpedo spun once, gathered his strength, then arched his back high and tight before kicking out with his hind legs. Vic continued to spur, his rhythm smooth and continuous despite the crazed beast trying to unseat him.

Then Torpedo went in for the kill and twisted midair. Tanya held her breath when Vic's backside lifted off the saddle at the same time his upper body pitched forward. How he managed to maintain his balance and continue to spur was pure magic. The crowd went wild when the buzzer sounded, and a surge of pride filled Tanya. She stuck her fingers in her mouth and let loose a shrill whistle. "Let's find your uncle and congratulate him."

"There you have it! Victor Vicario has won the saddle-bronc competition with a score of ninety!" When the applause died down, the announcer said, "Stick around, folks. The barrel-racing event begins in a half hour."

"You were incredible," Tanya said when she and Alex reached the cowboy ready area.

Vic's mouth curved a fraction. "What did you think, Alex? Was it a winning ride?"

Alex peeked up at Vic, then nodded.

"I better get going," Tanya said. "I'll meet you outside near the stock barn after my run."

Vic caught her arm when she stepped past him. His gaze burned into hers. "Be careful."

She quirked an eyebrow. "Don't you mean good luck?"

"That, too."

Tanya felt his eyes on her as she walked off, so she gave her fanny an extra little twitch. Blasted cowboy. One way or another she'd get him to kiss her again.

"YOU HUNGRY, BUDDY?" Vic asked Alex on the way to his truck in the parking lot. His nephew shook his head. Vic opened the door and tossed his gear bag inside, then set the truck alarm again and they returned to the arena.

"Mind if we stop to buy a snack?" They stood in the concession line and waited their turn. Then Vic purchased a soft pretzel and two bottles of water.

"Let's sit closer to the action." A lot of rodeo fans had left the arena, so he and Alex were able to find empty seats near the arena floor. He tore the pretzel in half and offered one part to Alex. He nibbled on the treat, every once in a while glancing up at Vic. The first barrel racer was announced. The cowgirl and her horse came racing out of the tunnel. Bits of dirt flew into the air as the horse's hooves pounded the ground. When Alex strained to see over the rail in front of them, Vic set him on his lap.

At first Alex stiffened, but after the second and third rider had competed their run around the barrels, his nephew had relaxed against Vic's chest. No doubt the kid was tired. If Vic had to guess, almost-five-year-olds were in their pj's by seven at night.

The announcer broadcasted a break in the action to allow rodeo workers to rake the dirt. Vic felt Alex's eyes on his face and wished he'd thought to sit the boy on the other side of his lap so he didn't have to stare at the scar.

"Ladies and gentlemen, we're down to our last rider of the night. Tanya McGee is from Longmont, Colorado. She and Slingshot will try to beat the winning time of 15.9 seconds."

Alex tore his gaze away from Vic's face and sat forward, his attention on the alley where Tanya and Slingshot would appear. A moment later she and the horse burst past the electronic eye.

Vic hadn't known he'd held his breath until Slingshot made the turn around the first barrel and raced toward the second one. There was something different about the way Tanya sat in the saddle, but Vic couldn't put his finger on it. Whatever adjustments she'd made, Slingshot appeared to handle them well. As they made the third turn, Slingshot nudged the barrel, but it remained standing and they headed for the straightaway, then disappeared down the alley.

"Look at that, folks, Tanya McGee and Slingshot finished with 15.3 seconds and that's good enough for first place!"

"Tanya won, Alex! She won!" Vic clapped his hands and Alex joined in. Instead of setting Alex on the ground, Vic carried him out to the corral, where Tanya walked Slingshot. Several cowgirls stopped to congratulate her, so Vic waited his turn. When Tanya was finally alone, he moved out of the shadows but paused when a cowboy approached her. The man looked a lot younger than Vic. Whatever he said made Tanya laugh. Vic's stomach burned with jealousy, propelling him forward.

He set Alex on the ground next to her. Keeping one hand on his nephew's shoulder, he offered the other to the stranger. "Victor Vicario."

The younger man shook his hand, his questioning gaze sliding back to Tanya.

"That was a hell of a ride, Tanya," Vic said. "You about ready to go back to the motel?"

The younger cowboy's face turned red. Then he tipped his hat and beat a hasty retreat.

"I thought we were taking Alex to see Dr. Harper."

Damn it, he was acting like a fool. "I guess in all the excitement I forgot."

"Did you see how well Slingshot ran?" Tanya spoke to Alex. "He was faster than the wind." Alex nodded. "Let me give Slingshot a rubdown before I put him in his stall for the night."

Tanya led the gelding into the barn while Vic and Alex waited outside by the calf corral. Until the cowboy had spoken to Tanya, Vic hadn't wanted to admit that he was emotionally involved with Tanya. But there was no denying he wanted more from her than to just share her bed. Why Tanya? Why now when he was chasing a title? Add his protective feelings toward Alex into the mix and the two could easily derail him from his goal.

Twenty minutes later the three of them climbed into Vic's pickup and headed away from the fairgrounds. He drove into town and parked in front of Dr. Harper's office. Ann, the receptionist, had left for the evening and Dr. Harper greeted them in the waiting room. "Hello,

Alex," she said. When Alex inched closer to Tanya, the doctor said, "Why don't you both come into the room with us?"

The four of them sat in child-size chairs around a small table. Dr. Harper pushed a basket of markers and a pad of paper toward Alex. "If you feel like drawing, go ahead," she said, then spoke to Vic. "How is everyone sleeping at night?" Everyone meaning Alex.

"Sleeping through the night." He glanced at Tanya and she nodded. Vic suspected the boy's sleep wasn't as deep and restful as his little body needed. In the time they'd been together, Alex hadn't cried out once in his sleep, and Vic assumed the boy had blocked out the day he'd been left alone in the apartment.

"I put together a list of activities and suggestions to help stimulate conversation between everyone." Dr. Harper nodded to Alex's drawing—a swing with two stick figures. "Playmates would be beneficial."

Playmates might be a problem if Alex continued traveling with Vic.

"I've also gathered some reading material, which will be helpful until you have the opportunity to visit another therapist."

"Thank you, Dr. Harper," Tanya said.

Alex pushed the markers away from him and stood. He looked at Vic, then at the door. He and his nephew had come a long way in reading each other's faces. "I guess we're ready to go."

Dr. Harper escorted them to the waiting room, where she handed a small fabric tote bag to Tanya. "My business card is in there. Feel free to call me if anything comes up."

After they left the therapist's office and got into the pickup, Vic said, "I think I remember passing a Chinese restaurant right before the turnoff for the motel."

"I like Chinese food," Tanya said.

"What about you, Alex?" Vic glanced in the rearview mirror, then lowered his voice. "He's asleep."

"Your nephew is a trouper," Tanya whispered.

Vic couldn't have asked for a sweeter kid to have to take care of. "You and Slingshot looked good tonight." He flipped on the blinker and moved into the other lane. "How'd you get him to run faster around the first barrel?"

"Fred gets all the credit. He suggested I let Slingshot pick his own pace as he approached the barrels. And it worked." She waved a hand in the air. "I really need a win tomorrow."

Vic grinned. "Are you looking forward to telling your stepfather he was wrong about Slingshot?"

She shook her head. "I needed the win tonight for me as much as for Slingshot."

"I don't follow barrel racing. Did you have a lot of success before…" He snapped his mouth closed. Maybe she didn't want to talk about her split with Billings.

"The car accident?" She sighed. "I was a decent barrel racer. But it wasn't about winning. I'd won a few competitions and that was fun, but I enjoyed the challenge of trying to beat my best time when I competed. I was doing really well when I had the accident and it's always bothered me that I couldn't leave the sport on my terms."

"Why did you wait so long to return to the circuit?"

"Rehab took over a year. Then Beau contested the divorce and—"

"Billings is an ass."

Tanya chuckled. "He wanted us to reconcile, but I knew he'd cheat on me again. Besides, Mason threatened to blow a hole through him if he tried to visit me at the horse farm."

"Sounds like your injuries were serious if rehab took that long."

"There were complications with my leg healing. Then I came down with pneumonia. It was rough. Mason and my mother both freaked out a little when I told them I was going back on the circuit."

"Which leg is it?"

She didn't favor either leg when she walked or climbed into the saddle. "My right leg. Didn't you feel the scars when…"

Vic gripped the wheel tighter at the memory of their lovemaking. He glanced across the seat. "I didn't notice." That was the truth. He'd been so caught up in the moment the first time.

"I'm not planning a second go-round in barrel racing. I just wanted a chance to retire on a good note. I didn't want my last memory of the sport to be connected with finding Beau in bed with another woman."

"If Slingshot keeps running like he did tonight, you have a good chance of racking up a few more wins."

They arrived at the Chinese restaurant. "What would you like?"

"Anything with chicken. And see if they have milk for Alex."

Vic went inside. The teenager behind the register rang up the order and told him it would be ready in five minutes. Vic doubted five minutes of breathing hot peanut oil would erase the scent of Tanya from his head. How could a woman smell so nice all the time? It didn't matter if it was the beginning of the day when she was fresh from the shower or the end of the day after she'd competed. She always smelled good. *You've been keeping your own company too damned long.*

While he waited for their food, Vic wondered if he could talk Tanya into sleeping in one of the double beds in his room. Saving money wasn't the issue. He was lonely. He'd been lonely for years, and it had never bothered him until he'd met Tanya. When he wasn't with her, the loneliness almost suffocated him.

"Thanks." He carried the food out to the pickup.

"Smells good." Tanya held the bags on her lap.

Alex stirred in the backseat. "You hungry, buddy?" Vic backed out of the parking space. "Hope you like Chinese food."

Vic drove one block, then turned into the motel and parked by a side entrance. "We might as well eat in my room."

They piled out of the pickup, Tanya carrying the food and Vic grabbing her and Alex's bags from the backseat. His room was on the first floor and when they stepped inside, he noticed the maid had straightened up the place.

"Why don't you use the bathroom first, Alex, then wash your hands?" Tanya said.

Vic sat on the bed and checked his messages while Tanya unpacked the food on the table in the corner. When Alex came out of the bathroom, Tanya set him in the chair. "Try a bite of everything. If you don't like it, you don't have to eat it." She glanced at Vic. "Mind if I use the bathroom next?"

"Go ahead." Vic pulled out one of the pamphlets Dr. Harper had suggested he look over from his back pocket and started reading it. This one talked about ways to make sure Alex knew that it was okay to talk about what happened to him. Reading the suggestions was one thing, finding the right moment to broach the subject with his nephew was another.

"I guess you like the stuff, huh?" The kid shoveled another bite of refried rice into his mouth.

Vic set aside the brochure and opened the carton of milk for Alex.

Tanya joined them, sitting next to Vic. He offered her the remote. "Watch anything you want."

"The news is fine," she said.

While they ate, Vic tried to figure out how to bring up the subject of all three of them staying the night in one room.

"Good job," Tanya said when Alex pushed his plate away from him. "Here's your fortune cookie." She unwrapped the treat and handed it to Alex. "If you break it open you'll find a tiny piece of paper inside."

Alex stared at the cookie, then handed it to Vic. He broke it apart and read the fortune inside. "Three is your lucky number."

"That's not exciting," Tanya said.

Alex climbed down from the chair and crawled onto the bed next to Vic then sprawled on his stomach facing the TV.

"I'll read mine." Tanya snapped open another cookie. "Seven is your lucky number." She laughed and then tossed a cookie to Vic. "Let's see what your lucky number is."

He swallowed a groan. "Your dream will come true."

Tanya's eyes grew round. "I see a big buckle in your future."

"Or this cookie just jinxed me."

She glanced at the clock on the nightstand between the beds. "Time for bed. Did you want Alex to stay here with you tonight or in another room with me?"

Vic glanced at Alex who'd already fallen asleep. "Why don't you two just stay here?"

Chapter Eight

Vic lay in the dark, staring at the ceiling in the motel room as he listened to Tanya's quiet breathing in the bed next to him. He hadn't expected her to take him up on his offer to share the room, but she did, insisting he shouldn't waste money. He'd neglected to mention that saving money wasn't the issue and he had plenty of cash in the bank.

Most of the time when the voice in his head analyzed his motives, he tuned it out. Tonight the darkness taunted him and he gave free rein to his conscience, admitting that he needed Tanya close for selfish reasons. When she was with him he didn't feel as unsettled around Alex. Her presence calmed his nerves. When he was alone with his nephew, the knot in Vic's stomach twisted tighter. He was never sure how to react to his nephew's looks. And there were so many looks—sad, worried, vacant. Vic ached when he considered the uphill battle Alex faced for years to come in dealing with his grandmother's abandonment and then being shuttled from foster home to foster home. And when he turned eighteen and graduated from high school—

if he didn't drop out before that—the state would push him onto the streets to live on his own. If Vic had a home or a stable job, he'd take Alex in, but there was no guarantee he'd win a national championship in December—shoot, he might get hurt and not even make it to Vegas. If he didn't win a buckle this year, he'd try next year and keep trying until he was too old to straddle the back of a bronc.

The sheets rustled in Tanya's bed and Vic rolled his head sideways on the pillow. She flung off the covers, and her quiet sigh floated into the darkness. A sliver of light spilled beneath the bathroom door, illuminating the room enough to make out the shape of her body. The sleep T-shirt she'd worn to bed rode up, exposing her thigh. A vision of her sexy leg wrapping around his waist flashed through his mind, and his body hardened. She rolled over, facing his way. Then she opened her eyes and their gazes clashed, neither blinking. Neither looking away.

After a few seconds she slipped from her bed and padded softly to the bathroom. He closed his eyes and tried to ignore his growing arousal. The shower in the bathroom came on. He gave up and moved across the room, turned the knob and stepped into the bathroom. He expected to find Tanya in the shower, not sitting on the toilet tank, her T-shirt hiked over her thighs, her pink panties peeking at him.

He leaned against the door—him in his boxer briefs—and stared at her. He didn't know what to say because he didn't know what was happening between them.

"What are we going to do about this?" she whispered.

"Do about what?"

She slid off the toilet tank and stood before him—not close enough that they touched but close enough that he could smell her. Feel her breath against his skin. She pressed her fingertip into the middle of his chest and dragged it over his nipple. He clenched his teeth.

"You want me, don't you?"

In case she had any doubts, he placed his hand at the small of her back and held her pelvis against his erection.

"Then why haven't you…"

"We had an agreement. I pay your expenses on the road in exchange for your help with Alex. This wasn't part of the deal."

She moved her finger south, grazing the waistband of his boxers. "What if we redefine the boundaries?"

He swallowed hard. Vic wasn't sure how long he could let her touch him and not reciprocate.

"This isn't part of the deal." She nuzzled his ear. "It's just…" She nipped his neck. "It's whatever we want it to be."

He could work with *whatever*. He clasped her face between his hands and kissed her deep and slow, then reached behind him and locked the door. Neither spoke when he tugged off her shirt and pushed her panties down over her thighs. Tanya knew exactly what he needed and she ground her hips against him. He wanted to go slow, but Alex was sleeping in the other room and he might wake up and need to use the toilet.

YOUR PARTICIPATION IS REQUESTED!

Dear Reader,

Since you are a lover of our books – we would like to get to know you!

Inside you will find a short Reader's Survey. Sharing your answers with us will help our editorial staff understand who you are and what activities you enjoy.

To thank you for your participation, we would like to send you 2 books and 2 gifts – **ABSOLUTELY FREE!**

Enjoy your gifts with our appreciation,

Pam Powers

SEE INSIDE FOR READER'S SURVEY

For Your Reading Pleasure...

We'll send you 2 books and 2 gifts
ABSOLUTELY FREE
just for completing our Reader's Survey!

YOUR READER'S SURVEY
"THANK YOU" FREE GIFTS INCLUDE:
- ▶ 2 FREE books
- ▶ 2 lovely surprise gifts

PLEASE FILL IN THE CIRCLES COMPLETELY TO RESPOND

1) What type of fiction books do you enjoy reading? (Check all that apply)
   - ○ Suspense/Thrillers
   - ○ Action/Adventure
   - ○ Modern-day Romances
   - ○ Historical Romance
   - ○ Humour
   - ○ Paranormal Romance

2) What attracted you most to the last fiction book you purchased on impulse?
   - ○ The Title
   - ○ The Cover
   - ○ The Author
   - ○ The Story

3) What is usually the greatest influencer when you <u>plan</u> to buy a book?
   - ○ Advertising
   - ○ Referral
   - ○ Book Review

4) How often do you access the internet?
   - ○ Daily
   - ○ Weekly
   - ○ Monthly
   - ○ Rarely or never.

5) How many NEW paperback fiction novels have you purchased in the past 3 months?
   - ○ 0 - 2
   - ○ 3 - 6
   - ○ 7 or more

YES! I have completed the Reader's Survey. Please send me the 2 FREE books and 2 FREE gifts (gifts are worth about $10) for which I qualify. I understand that I am under no obligation to purchase any books, as explained on the back of this card.

154 HDL GJZ7/354 HDL GJZ9

FIRST NAME | LAST NAME

ADDRESS

APT.# | CITY

STATE/PROV. | ZIP/POSTAL CODE

READER SERVICE—Here's how it works:

BUSINESS REPLY MAIL
FIRST-CLASS MAIL   PERMIT NO. 717   BUFFALO, NY

POSTAGE WILL BE PAID BY ADDRESSEE

READER SERVICE
PO BOX 1867
BUFFALO NY 14240-9952

NO POSTAGE
NECESSARY
IF MAILED
IN THE
UNITED STATES

Vic spun, pressing Tanya against the door, spreading her thighs apart with his knee. Her tongue slipped inside his mouth and he forgot all the reasons this was wrong.

"RISE AND SHINE, SLEEPYHEAD." Tanya ruffled Alex's hair.

The boy pretended to sleep, but she saw his eyelashes flutter when he tried to peek at her.

"Okay, go ahead and snooze, but your uncle's bringing donuts back for breakfast and if you aren't dressed when he arrives, I can't promise that we'll save any of them for you."

Alex's eyes popped open and his mouth twitched. *C'mon, Alex, smile. You can do it!* He rolled out of bed and went into the bathroom, leaving the door wide-open while he peed. When he came back out she pointed her finger and said, "Always flush the toilet and then wash your hands." She lifted him so he could reach the sink. "Use soap."

When he finished she gave him a clean towel. Then after he dried his hands, she moistened a washcloth and wiped the sleep from his eyes before patting down the stray hairs sticking up on his head. "You look very handsome today, cowboy Alex." She gathered her beauty supplies and packed them in her duffel bag.

Both she and Vic had risen at the crack of dawn. He'd used the restroom first, then split to get breakfast. And she'd taken her time dressing and putting on makeup. Neither brought up the night before, but the heat was there in every look they exchanged.

A noise in the hallway drifted under the door a moment before the lock opened and Vic walked in, carrying a white bakery box and a paper bag. His gaze skimmed over her—slowly—eyes warming. "I brought chocolate-covered and glazed. And a special one for Alex."

Alex peered into the open box and Vic placed the donut with colored sprinkles on a napkin, then removed a plastic bottle of milk from the bag and opened it for his nephew. "Before you eat the donut you have to eat a banana."

"They sell fruit at the donut store?" Tanya asked.

"I filled up the truck and bought it at the convenience store when I paid for my gas." He peeled back the banana and handed it to Alex, who ate it without protest.

"Thanks for breakfast." Tanya selected a glazed donut. "Better only eat one. If my hips get any bigger, Slingshot will object."

"There's nothing wrong with your hips." Vic's comment rolled over her like warm honey. "They're perfect." His gaze zeroed in on her fanny.

Tanya's face heated at the compliment. After she'd married Beau he'd never complimented her on her figure. *Since when do you care what a man thinks about your body?*

Since Victor Vicario had taken an interest in her, that's when. Good grief, she was losing it.

"We'd better hit the road. I want to make sure Slingshot warms up before we compete today." She washed her sticky fingers in the sink and helped Alex wipe off the sprinkles stuck to his lips.

Once they loaded their bags into the pickup, Vic drove to the fairgrounds. After he parked near the livestock pens, Tanya expected him to go off on his own with Alex, but her two favorite cowboys hung out with her and helped feed Slingshot. Alex held the bucket of oats while the horse stuffed his big nose inside and chowed down.

Vic walked off, then a few minutes later returned with an empty grain sack and gave Slingshot a rub-down. The horse soaked up the attention. "Barrel racing is back to its original time slot," she said. "Noon."

"You want to grab lunch before then?"

She shook her head. It was enough that Vic paid for most of her meals. She didn't want to take advantage of him.

"You're not worrying about your hips, are you?" he asked.

She flashed a sassy smile. "My hips have a mind of their own whether or not I worry about them." Once Slingshot finished the oats, she said, "Time for you cowboys to get lost." Reins in hand, she walked the horse over to the water trough. "I need to get this big guy ready to race."

"You want to check out the bulls?" Vic asked Alex. His nephew slid his hand into Vic's. "We'll stop by the alley later to wish you good luck."

She waved. Once they were out of earshot, she spoke to Slingshot. "What do you think of Vic?" The horse snorted. "Well, I like him." *A lot.* She enjoyed his company and she admired him for keeping Alex with him in the middle of his season when he could just as easily have left him in the group home.

She was under no illusions about where she stood

with Vic. The reason they were together was that he needed her babysitting services, but he wouldn't have made love to her a second time if he didn't care about her or like her. Time would tell if *like* turned into something deeper.

"Hey, big shot."

Tanya spun and came face-to-face with Beau. "Are you following me on the circuit?" He hadn't competed in saddle-bronc yesterday, so why was he in town? Then she noticed he wore a brace on his left knee. "What happened?"

"Pulled a ligament. I'm taking a few days off." He nodded in the direction Vic and Alex had walked off. "Didn't know Vicario had a kid."

"That's his nephew."

Beau narrowed his eyes. "Are you sleeping with him?"

"What do you care?" She should walk away and avoid an argument, but hey, she was only human and she liked the idea that Beau was jealous of Vic.

"I don't want to see you get hurt."

"Maybe you should have thought of that when you were screwing around behind my back."

"You know I still care about you."

Beau was telling the truth. He did still care—like a person cared about a pet he'd been forced to give up. "Vic and I are involved, that's all you need to know."

"You're with him because you feel sorry for him."

"I'm going to pretend I didn't hear you say that." She wasn't sleeping with Vic because she pitied him—that was so far from the truth it wasn't even funny.

"Don't you remember what drew you to me?" Beau quirked an eyebrow.

Tanya would never forget the night she and Beau met. She'd pulled into a gas station after the rodeo in Amarillo and he'd been talking on his cell phone, begging whoever was on the other end for a lift. She'd known who he was—he'd won the bronc-riding event that day. She'd nodded to him when she entered the convenience mart to pay for her gas. He hadn't given her a second glance—until she'd walked back outside and then he'd snagged her elbow.

"Hey, darlin'," he'd said. "You wouldn't by chance be heading to Lubbock next, would you?"

Beau had recognized her as a barrel racer, but if he was offered a thousand dollars, he wouldn't have been able to come up with her name. Then again, Beau wasn't any good at names—he cataloged the ladies by their boob size. "As a matter of fact, I am. Why?" She watched his face, fascinated by the pink tinge that colored his cheeks.

"I lost my ride."

She glanced across the parking lot. "What happened to your pickup?" He drove a newer-model Dodge Ram.

The muscle along his jaw bunched. "Someone borrowed it."

Tanya smiled—she couldn't help it. "Ah…pissed off another buckle bunny, did you?"

"Rebecca Robins."

Beau had looked so miserable—as if he honestly didn't understand why the woman had driven off with his vehicle.

"I bet she'll be waiting in Lubbock when you get there." Poor cowboy and his ego.

"Can I hitch a ride with you?"

"Sure." She held up a hand. "But only if you can tell me my name."

His mouth dropped open and she laughed. "Just kidding. C'mon." And that was how they'd met. Then Beau had entertained her all the way to Lubbock with tales of his adventures on the road and Tanya had been amazed at how easy it was to talk to the heartthrob. By the time they arrived at the fairgrounds and she'd dropped him off at his pickup, she'd felt as if she'd known Beau for years.

Their goodbye had been awkward—Beau's gaze had kept dropping to her mouth and after a few heated seconds he'd finally nodded to her and walked away. From then on, whenever he saw her, Beau asked how she was. Over time their chats grew longer and longer.

Maybe Beau had forgotten, but he'd been the one who'd done all the talking and Tanya had mostly listened. Then one night they ran into each other at a honky-tonk and after a few drinks, Beau made a pass at her and she caught it. It wasn't until after they'd been married several months that it occurred to her that Beau treated her like a friend, not a wife. Then she'd caught him cheating and the fantasy ended.

"I've got to take care of Slingshot." She entered the corral and walked over to the horse.

"Good luck today." Beau limped away.

That he wished her good luck surprised Tanya. Maybe he was finally growing up, too. As she saddled Slingshot, Beau's words echoed through her mind. Did she feel sorry for Vic? She was a sucker for the underdog—heck that was why she was riding Slingshot—Mason had given up on the horse. But no one was writing off Vic. Scar or no scar, there was no reason to pity the man.

But every time she saw him at a rodeo, he'd been alone—friendless. Then when he'd changed the flat tire on her trailer and she'd offered to buy him a cup of coffee, he'd driven away. She'd watched his truck until the taillights disappeared, then returned inside, more determined than ever to get to know him better. Once she understood his situation with Alex, she'd wanted to be there for him as a friend. But she'd made everything more complicated by sleeping with him, because now friendship with Vic wasn't enough.

Crap. Why was she drawn to such a complex, complicated man? There was no doubt in her mind the cowboy would break her heart.

"I won, Mom!" Tanya screeched into her cell phone ten minutes after she and Slingshot had won the barrelracing event by a fraction of a second.

"Honey, that's wonderful."

Tanya heard a voice in the background.

"Mason wants to talk to you."

"Tanya?"

"I won, Mason."

"Does that mean you're coming home?"

"Not yet." Good grief, couldn't he let her bask in glory for a few minutes at least? She wanted to see if it was luck that Slingshot had won or if he could run this way every time. And now that she'd gotten a taste of victory, she wasn't ready to call it quits. "As long as Slingshot can place in the top three, I'm going to keep him—" *and me* "—in competition." Tanya heard her mother speaking in the background and said, "Maybe I can squeeze in a trip home next month." Things might slow down by mid or late August and Alex would have been placed in a foster home by then. Even if Vic didn't need her babysitting assistance, she wasn't ready to say goodbye to him.

"Your mother wants to know how your leg is taking the stress," he said.

"It's fine. No pain at all. Please tell her not to worry. I promise I'm not pushing myself too hard." If the screws and plates were going to pop free, they'd have done so by now. "I'll call again in a few days."

"We miss you."

"I miss you guys, too. Give my love to Mom." Tanya ended the call and as soon as she slid the phone into her back pocket and turned around, a young brunette reporter shoved a microphone in her face. "Tanya McGee. What made you decide to return to barrel racing after your car accident?"

Whatever happened to "How does it feel to win?" She had opened her mouth to speak when someone touched her elbow—Vic and Alex stood behind her. She smiled, expecting their congratulations. What she heard left her speechless.

"Traffic's bad. We need to leave."

"But…" She glanced at the reporter, whose gaze

swung like a pendulum between Vic and Tanya. "Let me answer a few questions and then—"

"Suit yourself. I'll let you know where we stop for the night." Vic walked off, Alex holding his hand, his little legs pumping fast to keep up.

Oh. My. God. Vic was leaving her behind. Anger drowned out the excitement of her win. Fuming, she told the reporter, "I'm sorry. I have to go."

"Will there be a next time?" the reporter asked.

"You bet there's going to be a next time." She forced a smile, then walked Slingshot outside to the corral, where she unsaddled him and allowed him a drink of water. Across the lot she caught sight of Vic helping Alex into the backseat of his pickup. The traffic was bad—yeah, right. They had a few days to make it to Amarillo, Texas, for his next rodeo.

She gave Slingshot a quick rubdown. When she led him from the corral, she noticed Vic's truck now sat parked next to her pickup. He got out and walked over to her. "Is Slingshot ready to load?"

"Yes."

He opened the trailer doors and lowered the ramp for her. Then she escorted the horse inside. "Vic?" She caught him staring into space.

"Aren't you going to congratulate me on my win?" she asked.

"Congratulations," he said in a flat voice. She walked down the ramp and stood in front of him.

Hands on her hips, she glared. "What's the matter with you?"

"Nothing, why?"

"Well, for one thing you rudely interrupted me and the reporter. It's not like you to be mean." Beau had said mean things to her in the past, but Vic wasn't disrespectful.

His shoulders slumped. "I'm sorry. You're right, I shouldn't have interrupted." Then he removed his hat and looked her in the eye. "Congratulations on your win. You and Slingshot looked great out there." He stowed the ramp in the trailer and shut the doors before getting into his pickup.

So much for a victory celebration tonight. Tanya locked the trailer doors, then followed Vic out of the fairgrounds. As they left the city limits of Mesquite behind, she decided not to let Vic's bad mood dampen her spirits. She'd relish the victory even if she had to party by herself.

Chapter Nine

Vic parked in the lot behind the Amarillo National Center, where the Amarillo Tri-Sate Fair and Rodeo was taking place the second weekend of August. He glanced in the rearview mirror and watched Tanya pull her horse trailer up to the corral. He blamed the tension between him and Tanya on the piss-poor way he'd handled her win in Mesquite.

He'd been frustrated with his performance that night and had blamed his inability to focus on Tanya and Alex, which wasn't fair when his nephew had no control over his situation and Tanya was only doing Vic a favor by helping him take care of Alex so he could compete. If anyone was responsible for the mess he was in, it was his mother and sister. Their actions had set into motion the circumstances Vic found himself in. He'd believed he'd escaped the barrio and had left his sordid past behind when in truth he could never run from who he was or where he'd come from.

"Are you tired of all the rodeos, Alex?" He checked over his shoulder—his nephew was fast asleep. By now he'd expected to hear from Renee that they'd located a home for Alex. Twice he'd dialed her number, but something had stopped him from completing the call. Even though Alex never engaged in conversation, he was showing more facial expressions and nodding yes or shaking his head no when asked a question. And the vacant stares were becoming few and far between, which made Vic believe the boy wasn't thinking about the past as often. He gave most of the credit to Tanya's upbeat attitude with Alex, and her non-stop efforts to engage him in conversation.

In all the years Vic had rodeoed, this was the first time he'd traveled with anyone. Giving up his privacy hadn't been as difficult as he'd expected. He enjoyed having company when he drove and someone to eat with at the end of the day. He'd focused on his goal for so long that he'd shut himself off from feeling any emotion. Then a pint-size kid and a stubborn barrel racer showed up in his life and thawed the chunk of ice in his chest. Thinking about saying goodbye to them felt… uncomfortable.

Vic's phone beeped and he checked the number— Judge Hamel. If she was reaching out to him it must be important. "This is Vic."

"Victor, this is Judge Hamel. There's been a development in Alex's case."

He held his breath, anticipating the news that they'd found his nephew a foster home.

"Natalia's being paroled early from prison and she's asked the courts to give her custody of Alex."

He had a tough time believing his sister was that

eager to be a mother again. "How can she take care of him when she doesn't have a job or a place to live?"

"I don't know all the details, but Alex's social worker would like you to bring him to Albuquerque, where they'll evaluate the situation. When can Renee expect you?"

He couldn't think straight. "Why haven't they found a foster home for Alex?"

"Too many kids and not enough homes. For the time being Natalia may be Alex's best bet."

Natalia wasn't anyone's best bet.

"I've been following the rodeo standings. You moved up to eighth place. Maybe this will be the year you win in Vegas."

"I hope so."

"Don't forget to call Renee and let her know when you're coming to town."

"I will. Thanks." He disconnected the call. A lot of people hoped he'd make it to Vegas, but no one more than himself. Everyone wanted the poor kid from the barrio to succeed. Most people assumed he was riding for fame and glory, not because he needed to make things right with Cruz. Once he did that, only then could he get on with his life.

He glanced at his sleeping copilot. The little bugger had wormed his way into Vic's heart and he wanted to protect the boy from being hurt again. If Natalia believed she was ready to be a mother, she was delusional. His sister had dropped out of high school and had no formal training of any kind, which meant a minimum-paying job for her at best, and then who'd take care of

Alex while she was working? Where would they live—rather, who would they live with? Natalia wouldn't make enough money to pay for an apartment on her own. He had a slew of questions he wanted answers to before he left Alex in Albuquerque and drove away.

He spotted Tanya walking toward the truck, so he turned off the engine and rustled Alex's shoulder. "Hey, little man. Time to wake up. We're at the rodeo."

Alex yawned, then unsnapped the buckle on his safety seat and climbed out. Vic held the door open and took his nephew's hand as he jumped to the ground. When Alex saw Tanya, he pulled free and walked toward her. Tanya smiled, her eyes focused on Alex. Her smile was what had caught Vic's attention the first time he noticed her. She didn't just smile with her mouth—her eyes sparkled, making a person feel special. Important.

"Did you have a good rest, Alex?" She hugged him.

"How did Slingshot do on the road?" Vic asked. They'd driven the final three hours without stopping.

"Good. He'll be ready to compete tomorrow." She looked at Alex. "I bet you have to use the restroom."

"I'll take him." Vic grasped Alex's hand. "We'll meet you at the concession stand." Fifteen minutes later he and Alex found Tanya sitting at a table. The smell of fried food and popcorn filled the air.

"I think Alex and I will share a roast beef sandwich." Tanya looked at Alex. "Want to try a banana-berry fruit smoothie?" He nodded.

"Coming right up." Vic purchased their meals and they ate in silence. He figured Tanya was tired from driving. "I made a reservation at the Best Western two miles up the road."

"Give me a half hour to make sure Slingshot is settled in." She rose from the table and then waved Alex back to his seat when he tried to follow her. "You wait with your uncle, Alex. I'll be back in a little bit."

Alex's gaze followed Tanya until she disappeared in the crowd. "What do you say we take a look at the rabbit barn?" Alex nodded. Vic collected their garbage and dumped it into the trash can. Then they walked to the livestock barns. Twice he'd tried to bring up Alex's grandmother on the drive to Amarillo, but hadn't been able to find the right words to start the conversation.

Before they reached the bunny barn they crossed paths with an ice-cream truck and Vic decided now was the time to have that talk with Alex. "Two cones, one with sprinkles." After he paid for the treats, they sat on a bench in the shade.

"I'm real proud of you," Vic said. "It must have been pretty scary when your grandma left you all alone and didn't come back."

Alex stared at his cone. Then after a few seconds he nodded before taking another bite.

"I'm sorry I never came to visit you or your mom and grandma." Vic waved a hand in front of him. "Rodeo keeps me pretty busy, but that's no excuse. I promise to visit you more often after you go back to Albuquerque." Alex's eyes widened and Vic got the sense that the boy didn't want to return to Albuquerque.

"I bet you miss playing with your friends."

Alex stopped eating his treat. What if the boy didn't

have any friends? Vic pictured his nephew stuck inside an apartment day in and day out with nothing but a TV to entertain him. Would it be the same with Natalia?

Vic didn't ask what activities Alex had done with his mother because even before she'd been arrested she'd take off for months at a time with guys and leave Alex behind with their mother. Alex had never had a normal family life—then again, neither had Vic and his siblings. He wanted different for Alex. The boy deserved a mom who would hug him and put bandages on his scrapes and a dad who would throw a baseball with him in the yard.

Alex reached up and touched his sticky fingers to the scar on Vic's face. Their eyes met and Vic saw no fear in the boy's gaze—just sympathy. His nephew removed his hand, kissed his tiny palm, then patted the scar. Vic's heart exploded. "Thanks, buddy. It feels a whole lot better." He hugged Alex close, humbled by his show of affection and awed that a child who'd been neglected most of his life would possess any compassion for others.

"It hurt real bad when it happened, but that was a long time ago." Vic closed his eyes and the past flashed through his mind, his body jerking when he recalled the searing pain of the knife blade slicing through his face. He opened his eyes and found Alex watching him. "It was an accident, buddy." It was easier to stomach the lie than live with the truth—that his mother had intended to hurt him.

A burst of cold chilled Vic's blood. He should have asked the social worker if Alex had been abused by his grandmother. "Hey, buddy, I know you're not ready to talk yet and that's okay, but I need to ask you something really important. Did your grandmother ever hurt you?" He held his breath. After a moment Alex nodded. And Vic's heart dropped into his stomach. He lifted Alex onto his lap. "I'm sorry, buddy." Vic didn't ask what his mother had done to Alex. He knew. When his mother came down off her high, she'd ranted, thrown objects across the room and shoved her children against the wall.

"There you are." Tanya stopped in front of them. "I've been searching all over for you guys." She eyed the ice-cream stains on Alex's mouth. "I see you had dessert without me." Her smile faded when her gaze connected with Vic's. "I'm first out of the alley tomorrow."

"Okay. Let's head over to the motel and check in." Vic helped Alex off the bench and then the three of them walked out to the parking lot. Once Vic secured Alex in the booster seat and shut the door, Tanya spoke.

"Is something the matter?" she asked.

"I'll talk to you about it tonight after Alex falls asleep."

LATER ENDED UP being eight-thirty that evening. Once Vic was sure Alex was sleeping soundly, he motioned Tanya to follow him outside.

"Something's the matter," she said. "You've got that weird expression on your face again."

"Again?"

"The same one you wore when you and Alex were eating ice cream at the fairgrounds earlier."

They stood next to his truck parked in front of the motel room.

"I spoke with Renee when you were helping Alex with his bath."

"Have they found a foster home for him?"

"Not exactly."

"What do you mean?"

"Renee said it might be a while before the right home opens up for Alex."

"You can't keep dragging that poor boy around the country," she said. "He should be in preschool this fall."

Tanya wasn't telling Vic anything he didn't already know. He paced next to the pickup. "My sister's being paroled early." He released a ragged breath. "She'll be living in a halfway house with other women and their children. They have room for Alex there." Vic waited for Tanya to fire off questions, but she remained silent. "Renee wants me to bring Alex to Albuquerque as soon as possible."

"What about your next ride in Kansas at the Cowtown Pro Rodeo?"

"I'll have to scratch."

"When are leaving?"

"After we compete tomorrow, but…"

"What?"

Saying goodbye to Alex would be difficult, and he could use Tanya's support. "I was hoping you'd come with us." Before she had a chance to object, he said, "I could show you my old stomping grounds."

"What about Slingshot?"

"Can you find a place between here and Albuquerque to board him? I'll pay the fee."

Her expression softened. "Are you sure you want me to go with you? Your sister may not appreciate me knowing your family business."

"I don't care what Natalia thinks." He tangled with wild broncs for a living, but he didn't have the courage to handle a simple goodbye.

Because you know it's not going to be simple.

"Okay. I'll find a place to board Slingshot."

After Tanya went into the room, Vic stood for a long while outside and stared at the night sky. Leaving Alex in Natalia's care would be difficult, but once he left Albuquerque it would be the end of the road for him and Tanya. He'd asked her to help him care for his nephew, but until now hadn't realized he needed her healing touch as much as Alex.

"WHAT'S GOING ON?" Tanya asked as soon as Vic emerged from the supervisor's office at the downtown Albuquerque CYFD building.

He grasped her elbow and escorted her outside and across the parking lot to his truck. They'd left her pickup along with Slingshot at Mill Farms, a boarding facility an hour east of Dallas. He held open the passenger door for her, then slid behind the wheel, started the engine and flipped on the air-conditioning.

"I was hoping for a chance to say goodbye to Alex." She'd miss Vic's nephew once he was gone.

"We're coming back." He tapped his fingers against the door rest.

When he made no move to put the truck into drive, she said, "Talk to me, Vic. What's going on?"

"My sister refused to see me."

"Why?"

A harsh laugh burst from his mouth. "Hell if I know. You'd think she'd be grateful that I've been taking care of her son."

"Let's go for a drive." Tanya breathed a sigh of relief when he backed out of the parking spot and turned onto the street.

"I should have pressed charges against my mother when she attacked me." He blew out a harsh breath. "Maybe if I had, things would have turned out differently for me and Natalia."

"I don't understand why she's giving you the cold shoulder."

"I think she's mad I wasn't around more to protect her from our mother. Instead I chose to avoid home, hang out with my friends and try to pledge a gang."

"You don't seem like the gangbanger type."

"When you lose the sense of security that comes with a home and a parent, you turn to anyone willing to look out for you." He pulled into a Denny's restaurant. "I don't want to be too far away when Renee calls."

Eating would help pass the time. They went inside and the waitress seated them in a corner booth. They both ordered apple pie and ice cream. "Natalia said that Alex's father has been asking about him."

"What does the man do for a living?"

"Fixes cars at a collision center."

"Do you think he had anything to do with your mother's disappearance?"

"No. Hector doesn't want custody of Alex."

"Then why is he asking about his son?"

"My guess is that he's testing the waters with Natalia to see if she'll let him get in her pants again."

Poor Alex.

"After I went on the rodeo circuit, Natalia would call me every few months and ask for money. I offered to help her out, but I insisted she had to find a job. She refused look for work, so I didn't open my checkbook." He shrugged. "I figured any money I sent would be confiscated by my mother and used for drugs."

They finished their pie, then Vic stared into space. Tanya's heart ached for him and Alex and the mess they were in. His phone rang and she listened to the one-sided conversation.

"They're ready to talk to me," he said, slipping the phone into his pocket.

Tanya tossed her napkin aside. "Let's go."

They rode in silence back to the social services offices. When they walked into the building, Vic grasped her hand. "Come with me?"

"Of course."

"Renee, this is Tanya," Vic said when they entered the private office. "She's been helping me take care of Alex."

"Please, have a seat." Renee pointed to the chairs in front of the desk, her expression sober.

"What's the matter?" he asked.

"I just got off the phone with Officer Andrews."

"And?"

"I'm sorry, Victor. They found your mother's body near the fairgrounds. She died of an overdose."

Vic felt nothing but relief at the news that his mother was dead. Relief for his mother that she'd finally found peace after a life that had been torturing her for decades. Relief for his nephew; that the boy would never have contact with his grandmother again. Relief for himself. Maybe now he'd stop seeing his mother's face every time he felt the scar across his cheek.

"Officer Andrews asked that you call him when we're finished here."

Tanya squeezed his hands but remained silent—she knew not to waste her breath on condolences.

"Okay, let's talk about Alex," Renee said. "We observed Natalia's visit with Alex in the playroom through a two-way mirror." She shook her head. "Your sister didn't pay any attention to him. After a minute or two Alex went off and played with the toys by himself while your sister spent the rest of the time on her cell phone."

Not the heartwarming reunion the little boy deserved after being separated from his mother for so long. Tanya curled her fingers into a fist, wishing she could punch something.

"It's not surprising Alex didn't appear distraught when he'd first been found. I believe he's used to being ignored." Renee opened a file and scanned the first page. "According to the prison records, your mother never brought Alex to visit Natalia. What concerns me most is Natalia's lack of maternal instinct." She nodded to Vic. "And her refusal to visit with you. If we were to place Alex in Natalia's care, we'd expect you to check up on them, but I doubt she'd cooperate."

"What are you saying?" Vic leaned forward in his chair.

"At this time we don't believe it's in your nephew's best interest to go with his mother."

"What happens to Natalia if Alex isn't placed with her?" Tanya asked. Someone had to voice the question.

"She'll remain on probation and receive counseling. Hopefully she just needs time to decompress after being released from prison. We still believe it's best to reunite a child with their mother, so our goal will be to try again once Natalia has made sufficient progress."

"And Alex?"

"We don't have a foster family for him yet. While your sister is working on her issues, Alex will have to return to the group home." Renee narrowed her eyes. "Unless you're willing to keep him with you awhile longer."

Vic didn't hesitate. "I'll keep him."

Tanya lost a little piece of her heart to Vic. He was willing to watch Alex even though he didn't know if she'd be able to continue helping him.

"Great." Renee closed the file. "Before you leave town, Alex has an appointment with a therapist." Vic opened his mouth to speak, but Renee held up a hand. "Dr. Harper phoned me and offered her assessment after the two visits with Alex. She believes Alex is doing well in your care and that with time he'll begin talking again. Whatever you're doing with him, keep doing it."

"When does Alex see the therapist?"

"Tomorrow morning. I'm sorry, that's the best I could do on short notice."

"Is Alex ready to leave, then?" Vic stood.

"Actually one of our social workers took him to see a dentist. You can pick him up here at five o'clock."

"It was nice meeting you, Renee," Tanya said.

Renee's phone rang. "See you in a couple of hours."

When they left the social worker's office, Tanya said, "You could show me the neighborhood you grew up in while we wait."

"You sure you want to drive through the barrio? It's not pretty."

She smiled. "I'd love to see where you ran wild."

He chuckled.

"Vic?"

"Yeah?"

"What you're doing for Alex is pretty amazing." Vic was missing two rodeos to make this trip to Albuquerque.

They got into the truck and Vic waited until she buckled her belt. "If traveling with me and Alex becomes too distracting," he said, "feel free to go off on your own. You've already gone above and beyond what most people would do."

Go off on her own? "Do you want me to leave?"

"The truth?"

"Yes." She held her breath, hoping she was more than just a babysitter to him.

"I want you to stay."

"Good. Because I'd like to keep competing with

Slingshot." *And I don't want to say goodbye to you. Not yet.*

He pulled out his phone. "You mind if I call the police before we take off?"

"While you do that, I'll go back inside and use the restroom." She hopped out of the truck and walked off, leaving Vic privacy to discuss his mother's case.

It turned out there wasn't much to discuss. Andrews reiterated what Renee had said—that his mother had died of a heroin overdose. She'd been dead a few days when a delivery driver found her and reported it to the police. Vic gave the officer permission to have the morgue send his mother's body off to a crematory and agreed to pay for the service. And *no*, Vic would not be picking up his mother's ashes.

He disconnected the call and a minute later Tanya climbed into the pickup. He was grateful she didn't press him for details about the call. He backed out of the parking spot in front of the municipal building for the second time that day.

"What are you showing me first?" she asked.

"My childhood home." They drove for five minutes and then he turned down a street with old apartment buildings on both sides. Fast food bags, broken beverage bottles and other garbage littered the street. The landscaping had once been nice, but only tree stumps poked out of the dirt.

"After years of competing in small towns, it must feel surreal when you think about living here the first eighteen years of your life," she said.

"Once you leave a place like this, it's tough to return."

"You can't rodeo forever. What are your plans after you walk away from the sport for good?"

"I haven't thought that far ahead."

"Why not?"

"Because there's no future to plan unless I win the buckle this December."

Chapter Ten

"It was nice of you to buy the arm floaties for Alex so he could use the motel pool," Tanya said.

Vic remained silent, brooding. He'd been acting distant since they left Albuquerque two weeks ago—she suspected a combination of worry and exhaustion. They'd put over five hundred miles on the truck, competing in two different rodeo events.

Tonight Vic had placed first at the World's Oldest Continuous Rodeo in Payson, Arizona, and she and Slingshot had taken third in their event. First place had eluded her since the Mesquite rodeo and she wondered if that victory had been pure luck.

"Did you injure yourself?" Vic's dismount had been rough and she'd caught his wince this evening when he moved his shoulder the wrong way.

"No."

She snorted, keeping her eye on Alex, who sat on the steps in the shallow end of the pool and played with a plastic boat. "If you did get hurt, I doubt you'd tell anyone."

"Guys don't bellyache about their injuries."

"Wanna bet?" Beau had whined worse than a spoiled puppy when he stubbed his toe, never mind when he broke a bone. "If you're not in pain, then why are you so tight-lipped?"

His dark eyes swung her way. "You really want to know what's bothering me?"

Oh boy. She hoped she hadn't opened a can of worms. "Yes."

"I don't like that you think I go out of my way when I do something nice for Alex." His gaze sought out his nephew. "I'm not the hard-ass everyone believes I am."

She knew that, but others… "Maybe you give people that impression because you never smile or engage the other cowboys in conversation." Vic had an aura around him that flashed *keep your distance* like a neon sign. "If you want others to know the real you, then you should socialize with your competition."

"Doesn't matter anymore."

She changed the subject. "How have your talks gone with Alex?" Each night before they tucked the boy into bed, Tanya would leave the room and allow Vic and Alex time to chat in private. Vic was supposed to ask Alex questions the therapist had given him before they left Albuquerque. He'd been instructed to write down the answers—if Alex responded to the question. She'd snuck a peek inside the notebook the other day when Vic left it on the table—there had been no entries.

"Alex ignores me," he said.

Ouch.

"Maybe I got it wrong."

"Got what wrong?" she asked.

"Maybe Alex would be better off with my sister or in a group home."

"Why would you think that?"

"Alex has been around females all his life. He's not used to men."

"Don't give up on him, Vic. He'll come around. I know he will."

Vic released a harsh breath, then stood. "Be right back."

Tanya's gaze followed his muscular backside as he left the pool area and walked to their room. She glanced at Alex and caught him watching his uncle. Then his gaze swung to her.

"He's coming back." She smiled and Alex's lips curved upward a fraction. With a lot of love, Tanya was certain Alex would get through this rough patch and be okay. Then an image of the barrio flashed before her eyes and the hope dimmed. Even if Vic's sister took an interest in her son, what were the odds of Alex having a safe, happy childhood? Vic had tried to pledge a gang when he was in high school. Did that same future await Alex in the barrio?

"Think I'll see if Alex is willing to talk out here." Vic clutched the notebook.

"I'll take a shower while you two chat." She patted his shoulder. "Lighten up. You look like you're about to face a firing squad."

Vic waited until Tanya returned to the room and then he joined Alex at the other end of the pool. He sat on the edge, put his bare feet in the water and opened the journal. "Alex, that nice lady you talked to when we visited

Albuquerque wants you to answer a few questions." His nephew ignored him. "It would make me really happy."

Alex grabbed his toy boat and scooted closer.

"First question. Do you miss your grandma?"

Alex looked up at Vic for the longest time, never breaking eye contact. Then he shook his head. Vic recorded his answer in the notebook. "Do you miss your mother?"

Alex shrugged.

"Can you tell me the name of one of your friends?"

He shook his head.

"Did your grandmother ever take you to the park to play?"

Another no.

"Did your grandmother have friends visit the apartment?"

No.

"Were you frightened when your grandmother left you alone for such a long time?"

Alex stared at his boat, then finally bobbed his head up and down.

"You were very brave, Alex. I'm proud of you." He ruffled his nephew's hair. "What do you think happened to your grandmother?"

After several seconds, Alex shrugged.

"Do you think she got hurt and that's why she didn't come back home?"

Another nod.

Kids were so damned forgiving. Vic deviated from the list of questions. "Did your grandma ever teach you to dial 911 on the telephone to call for help?"

Alex shook his head.

The knowledge probably wouldn't have helped Alex. Vic doubted the apartment had a landline and Vic's mother had probably taken her cell phone with her when she left the apartment.

There were several more questions, but Alex had turned his back to Vic, so he changed the subject. "Do you think Tanya should give Slingshot a new name?"

No.

"So you like the name Slingshot?"

He nodded.

"I guess it fits him, but I was thinking he should be called Stinker."

Alex looked over his shoulder, and his innocent face tugged at Vic's heart. He didn't want to think about dropping him off at a foster home and then driving away.

"What do you want to do when you grow up?" After a moment of silence Vic asked, "Do you want to ride broncs like me?" Vic chuckled. "Your uncle's pretty awesome, isn't he?"

Alex smiled.

Vic basked in the warmth spreading through his chest. Maybe he and Alex were growing closer. "You don't have to answer me if you don't want to, but are you afraid to talk?"

Alex didn't answer.

Vic had a feeling there was a good reason his nephew kept quiet all the time. He took a stab in the dark. "Did your grandmother tell you not to talk?"

Alex's eyes widened, then he nodded.

"Was it okay if you whispered?"

He shook his head.

What the hell kind of punishment had Vic's mother threatened Alex with if he spoke out loud? He still hadn't told Alex that she was dead. He'd wait until Renee found a foster home for him. "Well, your grandmother isn't here and I promise you Tanya and I won't get mad if you talk."

Alex turned his back as if he didn't trust his uncle. "You know what?" Vic said. "Your grandmother is so far away she can't hear us even if we yell."

Alex spun toward him.

"You want to yell something out loud with me?"

Alex nodded.

"How about cheeseburger?" His nephew's mouth quirked. "Or pizza?" Then he named Alex's favorite drink. "Chocolate milk?" Vic bumped his shoulder into Alex's. "Let's shout chocolate milk on the count of three. One… Two… Three… Chocolate milk!" He laughed. "You have to yell, too. One more time." He held up three fingers. "Three… Two… One… Chocolate milk!" This time Alex joined him.

Vic hugged the boy.

"What's all the yelling about out here?" Tanya stood next to the chain-link fence, her gaze darting between Vic and Alex.

"We were playing the shouting game." Vic stared at the formfitting Western shirt Tanya wore. She loved bright colors that clashed with her hair and he loved the way the shirts showed off her feminine curves.

"Shouting game?" Tanya smiled.

Vic looked at Alex. "It's a new game we just invented."

"Next time, ask me to play, will you? I like to shout, too," she said.

Alex smiled at her.

"I'm hungry. Let's grab a bite to eat." Tanya turned away and shouted, "Chocolate milk!"

Alex giggled, then took Vic's hand and the two got out of the water. Tanya waited by the room for them. Their gazes connected and her smiling eyes made him feel ten feet tall.

"I'm very impressed, Mr. Vicario." She rose on her toes and kissed his cheek.

"Thanks," he whispered. Tanya's approval meant more to him than his win earlier in the day.

"THERE'S YOUR UNCLE." Vic pointed at the TV. He and Alex were watching the news coverage of the rodeo events earlier in the day and they were showing footage of Vic's ride. "If I'd dipped my shoulder just a tad more, my backside wouldn't have come out of the saddle."

Alex sat next to him on the bed, a pillow propped against the headboard. Vic got a kick out of the way the boy mimicked him.

"I think your uncle's getting a big head." Tanya didn't look up from the book she was reading—a training manual on horses.

"I hardly ever watch TV in my motel room." Vic tried to keep a straight face.

"Yeah, right." Tanya laughed.

"I think you're drunk on pizza," he said. They'd

eaten two hours ago and then stopped at a Dairy Queen for ice cream before returning to the room.

Tanya closed her book. "And I think it's Alex's bedtime."

Vic held his hand up and he and Alex exchanged a fist bump. "You heard the boss, amigo. Go brush your teeth."

Alex crawled to the bottom of the bed and slid off. When he went into the bathroom, Vic caught Tanya's attention. "I was hoping we could talk after he falls asleep." Alex had taken a big step today and Vic was still amped up over it.

"Sure." She set her book aside and then took her bottle of water and went to the door. "I'll be out by the pool."

Since the room was only a few yards from the pool, they could keep an eye on the room while they sat outside. When Alex came out of the bathroom, he stared at Tanya's empty chair.

"She's out by the pool. She'll be back in a while."

Alex crawled into bed beneath the covers and snuggled closer to Vic's side. Vic rubbed his back, feeling the tiny bumps along his spine. It was a miracle nothing bad had happened to the boy after his grandmother had abandoned him.

Vic turned down the TV and made a move to get off the bed, but Alex's hand clutched his leg, so Vic remained where he was a little longer. Ten minutes later the tight grasp on his jeans loosened and Alex fell asleep. Vic turned off all the lights except the one in the corner, then left the room.

Tanya sat on a lounge chair, facing their door. "Feels like the temperature dropped since supper." He pulled up a chair next to her.

"The weather app on my iPhone is predicting rain the next few days."

He'd asked to talk to Tanya, but the truth was he just liked being with her, whether they talked or not.

"I peeked in the journal when you were helping Alex with his bath," she said. "How did you get him to answer all those questions?"

"I don't know. He just nodded or shook his head to answer."

"That was a pretty big step for him." Tanya reached between them and grasped Vic's hand. "And you."

He squeezed her fingers. "I think I know the reason he hasn't talked."

"Really? What is it?"

"When I asked if his grandma liked the house quiet, Alex nodded. Then I asked if his grandma let him talk and he shook his head no."

Tanya sat up straight. "Vic. What if Alex believes his grandmother abandoned him as punishment for talking or making too much noise in the apartment?"

"Jeez. I hadn't thought of that. It's possible Alex might be afraid to talk around us because he thinks we'll leave him."

"The poor kid must be scared to death."

Vic pulled his hand free from Tanya's grasp and shoved his fingers through his hair. "When I take him back to Albuquerque I'll be just another person who abandoned him." He left his chair and paced between the table and the pool gate. "I can't keep him with me forever. I've already slipped in the standings."

"Do you hear yourself?"

He stopped pacing. "What?"

She raised her arms in the air. "You act like this is all about what's best for you." She pointed to their room. "You're not considering what's best for Alex."

"It's a hell of a lot more complicated than you're making it out to be." He didn't even want to think about starting another season on the rodeo circuit. He was tired. Burned out. And being with Tanya made him yearn to do something more...something better with his life.

"Does it matter where you are in the standings as long as you make it to the finals?"

Aside from pinching his pride... "No." He stared at the moonless sky. "Maybe Natalia is making progress in the halfway house and will want Alex with her."

"Do you really think they'll let Natalia take care of him?"

"That might be the only option." Vic looked away from the condemnation in Tanya's eyes. She couldn't make it any clearer that she believed he should drop his quest for a title this year and focus on Alex. But the stakes were too high. This might be his last chance to make things right with Cruz.

"I guess you'll have to take it one rodeo at a time and see how things go."

"Thank you for helping me care for Alex." He needed to say it—and hadn't said it enough.

"He's a sweet boy."

"It would be nice if he stayed that way," Vic said.

"Why wouldn't he?"

"My nephew doesn't come from good stock."

Tanya left her chair and closed the distance between them. "You're good stock, Vic."

"Don't let my rodeo success color your judgment of me. I raised my share of hell running through the streets of Albuquerque. I did a lot of things I'm not proud of."

"But you made it out of there and now you're a different man."

Vic thought he'd left his past behind him—until he'd gotten the call about Alex. "Maybe I should have stayed in Albuquerque." Had he been a fool to believe each eight-second ride would carry him further and further from his past? It had taken just one phone call to rip away the thousands and thousands of miles he'd already covered chasing a title.

"If you hadn't left," Tanya said, "you never would have pursued rodeo and you'd never be this close to winning a national title. And Alex wouldn't have an uncle to look up to. You're a walking, talking example of succeeding in spite of your past."

What Tanya said sounded pretty, but… "I'm no better than my sister or mother. I abandoned Alex, too, by keeping my distance from all of them." But if he hadn't turned his back on his hometown, he would have joined a gang and, who knew, maybe he'd have gotten himself killed by now. A dead uncle was no good to Alex.

Vic thought back to the days he'd hung out with his best friends, Cruz and Alonso. Of the three of them Alonso Marquez had the brains to make something of himself and his life. Vic had nicknamed him the *negotiator* because he tried to talk guys down from fighting. Maybe if Alonso had been around on that fateful night years ago, Vic would never have carried out his plans. Until Vic's sister had been raped by the leader of the Los Locos—the very gang Vic had been pledging—he'd hadn't believed he was capable of violence. He'd demanded the jerk do right by Camila, and when the leader had laughed in his face, Vic had wanted to kill the bastard.

Years of resentment toward his mother, the unfairness of life, struggling every day to stay alive in the barrio, watching other guys his age find a way out when he couldn't had festered in him for years. That night his rage had exploded, scaring the crap out of Vic. If Cruz hadn't wrestled the gun from his hand, Vic would have been the one thrown in prison.

"Vic."

He blinked away the memory and focused on Tanya's blue eyes.

"You're here now," she said. "Taking care of your nephew when he needs you the most. That's all that matters."

"I should have known my mother would abuse Alex. She's been a drug user most of her life. By the time I left town there was nothing left of the mother I knew as a little kid." Hell, if Vic had ever felt anything close to love for his mother, he couldn't remember.

"Try not to worry about Alex. He's safe with us."

Safe for how long? The road was no place for a little boy, but neither was a group home. He tried to envision a future after rodeo. Where would he live? What would he do to support himself? But the biggest question that kept him awake at night… Would he be able to take care of Alex or would Alex be better off in a foster home with two parents?

Tanya tugged his shirtsleeve. "I was wondering if we'd have time to swing by Fairlie, Texas, on Monday. They're holding a free barrel-racing exhibition and I'd like to get in a couple of practice runs with Slingshot before we compete next weekend. But I understand if you'd rather just get to Oklahoma and rest a few days before the Will Rogers Memorial Rodeo."

Vic didn't want to sit around a motel room and think about how Tanya was getting under his skin and how difficult it would be to part ways with Alex. He was already having trouble picturing the three of them eventually going their separate ways.

"I think we can swing it."

"Thank you." Tanya wrapped her arms around his neck and kissed his cheek. Before she pulled away, he turned his head and their lips met. He moved his mouth over hers slow and easy before sneaking his tongue inside, showing her without words how much he wanted her.

Tanya pulled away first. "I better see if Alex is still sleeping."

Vic watched Tanya return to the room, wishing he could make time stand still.

Chapter Eleven

"This place is packed," Vic said when he and Alex met up with Tanya in the parking lot of the outdoor arena in Fairlie, Texas.

"Places like this draw big crowds that cater to people who love barrel racing but can't afford to travel to the larger rodeos."

Tanya had arrived an hour before Vic and Alex, and had already put Slingshot in a stall, where he was resting. "I race in a half hour." She pointed to a concession stand. "I'll have lunch after the race, but if you two are hungry go ahead and eat without me."

"We'll grab a snack and wait to eat with you later," Vic said.

Tanya crouched in front of Alex. "Will you cheer for me and Slingshot?"

He nodded.

"I want to hear you shout Slingshot's name really loud when we race around the barrels." She tapped her finger against the end of his nose, then glanced up and caught Vic studying her, his eyes soft and dark. When he stared at her like that, she almost believed they were a couple—for real and not just until they found a home for Alex.

"Be careful," Vic said.

"I always am." She returned to the horse stalls beneath a covered section of the arena. The shade provided relief from the heat, but it was close to ninety-six degrees and Tanya's Western blouse stuck to her sweaty back. "Hey, big guy." She stepped into the stall and patted Slingshot's rump. "You ready?" He nudged her shoulder with his nose and she scratched his ears.

"I'm going to give you a lot of lead this afternoon, so don't get cocky and cut the corners too sharp. I know you can beat fourteen seconds." She rubbed the ache in her calf, then bent at the waist and stretched the muscle. She was beginning to feel the affects of traveling on the road day after day. The long hours behind the wheel were taking a toll on her leg, and the hot baths each night in the motel room no longer relieved the constant throb in her bones. She was pushing herself too hard—exactly what Mason and her mother feared would happen. But she wasn't ready to quit—not yet. She'd stick with it until the pain made it impossible to compete or until Vic no longer needed her help with Alex. She backed Slingshot out of the stall and hitched him to the center post, then gave him a rubdown.

Slingshot stamped his hoof. "Easy, big guy." When she considered her motivation for returning to the circuit, she admitted that she'd felt as if Beau had robbed her of her career.

After they'd been married a few months, he suggested that she quit the circuit and help Mason train horses. Money was tight and Beau needed her paycheck to cover his entry fees until he climbed out of his slump. She'd refused, claiming her career was as important as his, but in the back of her mind she wondered if he'd only married her hoping she'd support him financially. They'd gotten into a huge argument and had gone their separate ways on the circuit. Once she'd cooled down and could think straight, she'd come up with a compromise that would allow her to ride half the year and train horses for Mason the other half. She'd hoped that Beau would realize the sacrifice she'd been willing to make for him...for them. And he showed his appreciation by sleeping around behind her back. The night of her car accident Tanya had been more upset with herself than Beau. In the back of her mind, she'd always known Beau had been using her—she just hadn't wanted to accept it until she was forced to when she found him in bed with a buckle bunny.

You're allowing Vic to use you like Beau did.

The voice in her head startled Tanya. Yes, she was helping Vic take care of Alex, but she was receiving something in return. Vic was paying for her food, lodging, gas for her pickup and Slingshot's entry fees and boarding. If anyone was getting the better end of the deal, it was her. She shut the door on her thoughts. Today was all about preparing for next weekend when she had the best possible shot of landing in the money.

She walked Slingshot to the alley, stopping in a patch of shade to check his tack, making sure the saddle was snug, and then they entered the line to wait for their turn. Several yards in front of them stood a black gelding whose saddle was adorned with enough bling to rival the afternoon sun.

"You don't care about fancy rhinestones, do you, boy?" she whispered in Slingshot's ear. Once the cowgirl up ahead climbed onto her horse, Tanya turned her thoughts inward. Today she intended to give Slingshot permission to go as fast as he wanted when he approached the first barrel. She had to find out—maybe the hard way—if she could remain in the saddle. If she couldn't, then she was back to square one with the stubborn horse.

The black gelding took off down the alley and burst into the arena. From Tanya's vantage point she saw her competitor navigate the turns and straightaways with ease and in no time at all the cowgirl and her rhinestone horse were making a sprint for the finish line. As soon as they broke the electronic barrier, Tanya glanced at the clock—an even fifteen seconds.

"Okay, big guy. No guts, no glory." Tanya swung into the saddle and then checked the stands. It took her only a second to find Vic and Alex. Both waved at her. "Win for Alex, Slingshot."

She switched her attention to the man at the end of the alley. He signaled that the timers had been reset and she was cleared to take off. She leaned forward and tapped her heels. Slingshot bolted, his first strides more powerful than she'd experienced before and adrenaline made her heart pound. *C'mon, Slingshot. You can do this. Beating fifteen seconds is nothing.*

As they raced toward the first barrel, Tanya pulled slightly on the reins, so Slingshot would approach at an angle. He didn't respond to the signal. Instead he ran in a straight line, barely applying the brakes as he turned. Tanya slid in the saddle, but she hung on. Her hat flew off, however. Had this been a sanctioned barrel-racing event, she'd be fined twenty-five dollars for losing her hat.

Slingshot took the second turn just as fast, and Tanya's leg bumped the barrel. Luckily the drum wobbled but remained upright. A moment of panic hit her when Slingshot veered toward the third barrel. He was going too fast to make the turn. She braced for a collision, all the while wishing Alex wasn't watching. At the last second Slingshot panicked and planted his left hoof less than a half inch from the barrel. Tanya's body jerked forward and she dug her knees into the horse and clenched her abdominal muscles. The effort saved her from flying through the air. Slingshot raced for the alley with a final burst of energy as he passed through the electronic timer. Before Tanya pulled back on the reins, Slingshot was already slowing and a pit formed in her stomach.

She hopped off his back and walked him behind the stands, where she could study his gait. He was stepping gingerly on the left front hoof. "You don't know when to stop, do you?"

Slingshot blew air from his nose. Despite coming up lame, the showoff knew he'd run a near perfect route. "Go ahead and gloat," she said, keeping an eye on his leg. "But you're going to pay a high price for not following my instructions." She led him to his stall for a drink of water, then signaled a local vet, who remained on the premises during the rodeo.

"What can I help you with?" The older man's kind blue eyes squinted at Tanya.

She introduced the vet to Slingshot and removed the horse's saddle. "It's the front left leg. He planted hard when he came around the barrel."

The vet took the reins. "Let's put him in the corral where I can get a better look."

"I'll be there in a minute." Tanya dropped the saddle on the ground and rubbed her watering eyes.

"What's wrong?"

She jumped at the sound of Vic's voice. "Nothing." She sighed. "Everything." Pasting a smile on her face, she ruffled Alex's hair. "What did you think of Slingshot? He was pretty fast today, wasn't he?"

Alex nodded, then looked up at Vic.

"You want to tell her?" Vic said.

"Tell me what?" Her gaze swung between the males.

Vic nudged Alex. "How many seconds did I say?"

"Thirteen." Alex smiled.

"And two-tenths. You're in first place," Vic said.

Tanya swiped at a tear that escaped her eye. "Go figure Slingshot would run his best time ever, then come up lame."

Vic frowned. "What happened?"

"He's favoring his front leg. The vet's in the corral with him right now."

Her gaze slid away from Vic's. They both knew what this meant—she and Slingshot had come to the end of their road together.

Vic straightened his shoulders. "Let's see what the vet says."

"I'M PRETTY CONFIDENT it's a soft tissue injury, but an ultrasound will be needed to see if surgery is required to repair the flexor tendon." The vet patted Slingshot's neck.

Vic curled his fingers into his palms as if making a fist could keep his panic from escaping his body.

"I can give him medication to help with the swelling and a shot for the pain, which will make him more comfortable riding in the trailer."

Tanya's lower lip trembled and Vic shoved aside his own worries. He put his arm around her shoulders. "He's a strong horse. He'll come back from this injury." *Maybe*. It would take a lot of therapy, money and a good dose of luck to get Slingshot healthy enough to compete again.

"Where's home?" the vet asked.

"Longmont, Colorado." Tanya's voice broke.

Alex hugged Tanya's leg when tears spilled from her eyes.

Vic felt helpless, wishing he knew how to make her feel better and how to stop the dread pumping through his bloodstream. He should never have agreed to this practice run today, but Tanya had been so excited and he'd wanted to make her happy. If they'd driven straight to Oklahoma, Slingshot wouldn't have gotten injured and the three of them would continue to travel together.

The vet handed Tanya a plastic prescription bottle. "Give him two every six to eight hours during the trip home."

Home. The word pierced Vic like a bullet between

the eyes. He didn't have a home. But Tanya did and her people were waiting for her return.

What about Alex?

Vic stared at the top of his nephew's head and thought his chest might explode from the churning emotion trapped inside. Images of his childhood flashed before his eyes; only it was Alex's face he saw, not his own. He couldn't let Alex return to Albuquerque and live in the group home.

Maybe he couldn't let him go at all.

The thought jarred Vic, but after the initial shock he realized he'd been preparing for this moment from the first time he met his nephew. No one would look out for Alex the way Vic would. And there was no teacher back in the barrio like Maria Fitzgerald to take Alex under her wing and help him escape the gangs. Vic was Alex's only way out.

The circuit was no place to raise a kid. Vic had seen his competitors try to take their families on the road year-round. Living out of a motor home and home-schooling children could be as stressful as dodging trouble in the barrio. But unless Vic had a nine-to-five job and a decent place for Alex to lay his head every night, social services wouldn't grant Vic custody of his nephew.

The only way Vic could find permanent work and settle down was if he retired from rodeo. And right now retiring was out of the question. "Tanya, let the doc take care of Slingshot while we discuss what to do next."

Tanya took Alex's hand and walked across the parking lot to Vic's pickup. Vic remained behind. "Doc," he said. "I'm taking care of the bill."

The vet nodded. "It's best to get this horse off the road as soon as possible so the injury doesn't get any worse."

That meant Vic and Tanya would have to part ways today. And damned if he was ready to say goodbye to her. He caught up with the pair and then drove to Don's Hot Dogs and parked next to the play area for kids in front of the restaurant. "You and Alex grab a table by the swings and I'll order our food."

A million thoughts raced through Vic's head as he stood in line at the order window. What kind of goodbye would this be with Tanya—a forever goodbye or a see-you-down-the-road goodbye? He needed time to figure out if what he felt for her was real or all twisted up with sexual attraction and gratitude for her help with Alex.

Tanya was the first woman ever who'd made him ponder the future. Until he and Tanya had made love, Vic had never allowed himself the luxury of planning a future after rodeo. All these years he'd focused on his next ride and then the one after that and the one after that. He'd dedicated his life to chasing a trophy and nothing else had mattered.

"Three dogs, a diet cola, a root beer and…do you have milk?"

The pimple-faced teenager shook his head. "A bottle of water, then."

"That it?"

"For now." Vic pulled his wallet out of his pocket.

"Twenty-one sixty-two."

He took his change and stepped away from the window while he waited for his order. He had a clear view of the playground where Tanya was pushing Alex on the swing. The kid must have said something out loud, because Tanya laughed. She was a strong woman and Vic admired her for putting on a brave face for Alex when he knew she was still crying inside about Slingshot's injury. He gave Tanya most of the credit for helping Alex come out of his shell and worried that the boy would shut down again if she left them.

Vic wanted to believe Alex would be fine if left alone with him, but what if the boy wasn't? Alex had just begun talking a little—what if he clammed up again. Talk or no talk, returning Alex to Albuquerque was out of the question. No matter that his sister was trying to get her act together, he didn't trust Natalia to take good care of her son and Alex was too young, too vulnerable to stand up to anyone who mistreated him. As much as he wished his sister would make Alex a priority in her life, Vic knew it would never happen.

How will you make Alex a priority if he stays with you?

He wouldn't. The sad truth was that rodeo would come first—for the next few months.

"Number seven-thirty-five."

Vic handed his claim ticket to the teenager, then carried the tray of food and drinks to the table. Tanya stopped the swing and she and Alex joined him. They ate in silence. Then after a short time Alex pushed aside his half-eaten hot dog.

"Are you full already?" Tanya asked.

"We shared nachos and fry bread in the stands at the rodeo," Vic said. When Alex kept fidgeting, Vic pointed to the playground. "You can play if you want, but don't wander off."

Alex joined a group of kids digging in the tire sandbox. "Doesn't look like you're hungry, either." Vic nodded to the uneaten food in front of her.

She shook her head. "I'm sorry."

"You don't have to apologize."

"If we'd stuck with your itinerary, Slingshot wouldn't be hurt right now."

"He might have pulled up lame in the next rodeo." The horse had a mind of his own and Vic doubted any amount of training or practice would tame his wild streak. Some animals weren't meant to be anything but wild and free. "What will you do with Slingshot?" He knew without asking, but he had to hear her say it; otherwise he wouldn't accept the truth.

"Take him back to Red Rock. Let him be a boring old ranch horse. Mason won't mind him taking up space in the barn, if it means I'm back training Appaloosas for him."

"You don't have to stop competing. I'll buy you another horse." He had the money in savings.

"Why?"

"Why what?"

"Why are you offering to buy me a horse? Is it because you care about me or because you need my help with Alex?"

"What if I said both?"

"Then I'd appreciate your honesty."

Vic more than cared about Tanya. He liked her—a lot. He worried about her. Wanted to be with her all the time. His every other thought had something to do with her. He wanted to feel more for her, but he couldn't go that far—not while he was pursuing a buckle.

"You might not be the womanizer that Beau is, but you two share one common trait."

"What's that?"

"Your careers are your number-one priority. Everyone and everything stands behind rodeo."

He opened his mouth to object, but she waved him off. "Don't worry. I'm not upset. You didn't promise me anything when we started on this journey together and it was naive of me to believe that you might see me as more than a babysitter, especially after we slept together."

Vic grasped her wrist. "I do have feelings for you, Tanya." He held her gaze, wishing he could be a better man for her. A man she deserved. "You're the first woman who's made me think about the future and where my life is heading." Her eyes begged him to say more… "I can't make any promises because I don't know how things are going to end this year."

"I get that you don't have time for personal relationships, but is a buckle more important—" her gaze swung to Alex "—than your nephew?"

"You don't understand." He released her wrist.

"Then make me understand."

Tell her the truth. Then she'll be glad to part ways. "A friend of mine spent twelve years behind bars because of me."

Tanya didn't say a word and Vic swallowed hard before continuing. "When my older sister confessed that a gangbanger had raped her but she was keeping the baby, I wanted the father of my sister's baby to step up and take responsibility for them. My friend Cruz tried to talk me out of confronting the guy, but when he couldn't he went with me."

The next part of the story wasn't as easy to tell. "I got into a heated argument with the guy because he didn't give a crap about Camila or the baby. I turned to leave but stopped when he mocked me for not defending myself against my mother and allowing her to mark my face."

Vic had never been so humiliated as he'd been that night when the gangbangers laughed at him. "I pulled a gun from the waistband of my pants. Cruz wrestled it from my grip, but it went off in his hands and the bullet hit the gang leader in the shoulder. Cruz went to prison for attempted manslaughter."

"That's horrible, Vic. But I don't understand what that has to do with you wanting to win a buckle."

"I never intended to rodeo. Cruz was supposed to join the circuit a few weeks after the shooting. Instead he sat in a prison cell. I robbed him of his career, Tanya."

"I don't believe it," she whispered. "All these years you haven't been riding for yourself. You've been riding for Cruz?"

"Cruz was destined to be famous in the sport, but I stole his future from him. He wasted his best years sitting behind bars. He deserves that championship buckle."

"What happens if you don't win this year?" Her sympathetic gaze socked him in the gut.

"Then I start over again next year."

"And now you have Alex to worry about." Tanya nibbled her lower lip, then sucked in a deep breath and looked Vic square in the eye. "If you're determined to win in Vegas this year, then you can't have any distractions."

"What are you saying?" Was she offering to travel with him and Alex?

"Alex can stay with me at Red Rock while you finish out the season."

Chapter Twelve

Tanya stood in the shadows of the horse barn at Red Rock and watched Vic say goodbye to Alex. Crouched in front of his nephew, Vic tried to look him in the eye, but Alex stared at the ground. Did Vic have any idea how difficult this goodbye was for the boy? He'd become Alex's rock—the superhero who'd rescued him.

Now that Tanya understood the real motivation behind Vic's obsession with winning a national championship, her heart ached for him and the heavy burden he carried. She'd like to believe Vic had taken her into his confidence because he cared for her—maybe even loved her a little bit. But the confession she yearned for remained locked inside him.

"What's going on between you and Victor?" Mason stopped by Tanya's side. "I saw the way he looked at you earlier. You're more than friends."

"I'm a big girl, Dad. I've been married and divorced. I don't need a lecture." She didn't mean to snap at him, but she was miffed at having to leave the circuit with Slingshot.

"I'm sorry," he said.

"No, you're not." She shifted her gaze to him and caught his wince. "You're happy Slingshot pulled up lame and I had to come home."

"Wait just a minute—"

"Maybe you're not *happy* that a horse injured itself, but you and Mom are relieved I'm not riding anymore."

He exhaled a sharp breath. "Yes, we're both glad you made it home without injuring your leg. Maybe if you'd explained to us why it was so important that you compete again, we could have been more supportive, but you just packed up the trailer, loaded Slingshot and took off."

"It had to be that way because you and Mom would have given me the guilt trip and I would have caved in."

"A parent's job is to make his child feel guilty."

For the first time Tanya noticed Mason's stooped frame. He'd always been a strong, big-boned man with a larger-than-life personality, but today he appeared shorter, slimmer, not as imposing. He looked all of his sixty-four years.

"I suppose me and your mother have been a little overprotective of you since the accident."

"A little?"

"Try to understand, Tanya. Your mother had already lost the love of her life years earlier. And you weren't there to see her face when the Nevada State Patrol called the house at 3:00 a.m. to inform her that you'd been taken to the hospital." He shoved his fingers into his jean pockets. "Some kids—" he nodded to Alex across the driveway "—go their whole lives without a parent's love."

She hadn't meant to make Mason feel bad. "I appreciate how much you and Mom care, but it's always bugged me that my career ended so abruptly. I never got a chance to see just how good I could be."

"Did you expect to return to the circuit and be competitive after suffering that kind of injury?"

"No, but I wanted to go out on a better note." She didn't want her last memory of rodeo being the night she'd caught Beau cheating on her. If she hadn't been sobbing and hysterical, she wouldn't have been speeding. Swerving at eighty-five miles per hour to avoid hitting the coyote had landed her flipped over in a ditch. Fortunately she'd worn her seat belt. "When I saw Slingshot, I thought he was just like me. Eager for one more go-round."

"After his injury heals, are you returning to the circuit?"

"No." She'd leave on a win. Besides, it wouldn't be the same without Slingshot.

"So what are your plans, then?"

"What do you mean? I'm staying here and training horses."

"What about Victor?" Mason's eyes swung toward the house. "I'll never forget the first time your mother looked at me, and it's the way you're looking at Victor right now."

Was it that obvious she'd fallen hard for the cowboy?

"I knew when I'd proposed to your mother that your father would always have her heart, but I was willing to settle for second best, because she cared about me.

We were friends before lovers. And I'd been lonely for a long time. The idea of a family appealed to me."

"Why didn't you and Mom have a child of your own?"

"Your mother didn't want one." He shrugged. "You and I got along well and we grew closer, so it didn't bother me that we didn't have more kids. But it made things more difficult for you."

That was the truth.

"When did my mother fall in love with you?" Tanya asked.

"It was the night of our fifth anniversary. I took her into town for a steak dinner like I did every anniversary. But that night when we danced, there was a different look in her eyes and I knew."

Tanya hugged her stepfather. "My father would approve, Mason. You're a good man." And so was Victor. Who would love him and take care of him?

"Whatever you decide to do about your cowboy out there, your mother and I will stand by you."

"You don't even know the whole story, Mason."

"But I know you and you wouldn't be with Victor if he wasn't a good man."

"Thank you for saying that." Tanya didn't want to accept the possibility that Vic and Alex might not be in her future.

"I put a call in to Ramona," he said. Ramona Baxter was the local vet. "She'll be out later to take a look at Slingshot."

"Mason." She snagged his shirtsleeve. "Thank you for letting Alex stay with us."

"Are you kidding? Your mother's excited to have the little guy running around the place."

"He's a good boy who's been through a lot."

"Maybe you can tell us his story later. Right now it looks like Victor is ready to hit the road."

Tanya glanced across the driveway.

"Better give him a proper send-off." Mason winked and retreated farther into the barn.

Taking a deep breath, Tanya left the barn and walked over to Vic's truck. "Alex, I bet Nana Jean has some cookies for you in the kitchen."

"Be good for Tanya, Alex. I'll stop by and visit real soon."

Alex still wouldn't look at Vic, but he flung his arms around Vic's leg, held on for a few seconds and then raced up to the house.

Vic shuffled his feet and glanced everywhere but at Tanya. "Alex has plenty of room to play here."

"We'll make sure he doesn't get near the horses. I promise he'll be safe with us." Images of Vic driving from rodeo to rodeo alone, checking into a motel room alone and eating alone, played through her mind, and her throat grew tight.

He pulled his wallet from the pocket of his jeans. "I'll leave one of my credit cards with you in case Alex needs anything. Use it for food or clothes." He held out the card. "Will you get a birthday gift for him from me? It's on the twenty-seventh."

"Can you make it back for his birthday?"

"I've got a ride that weekend." He offered the credit card again. "Throw him a party. I'll cover the expenses."

"And who's going to come to his party?"

"Maybe the ranch hands have kids who'd show up."

She pushed the credit card away. "Keep it. I'll find something special to do on his birthday." Couldn't Vic see that she'd do anything for him? But he'd never find peace with himself if he didn't finish the quest he'd embarked on years ago. And if he never found that sense of peace...if he never put the past to rest...then there could be no future for them. "Don't forget to call him on his birthday." She'd text him a reminder when she woke up that morning.

Vic slid the credit card back into his wallet. "You might need this. It's the insurance card Renee gave me in case Alex gets hurt or has to see a doctor."

She took the card and put it in her pocket. Tanya had spoken to Renee at length after social services approved Alex living at the farm. Tanya had promised to find a therapist for Alex while he was there, and Renee agreed that it was best for Alex to settle down in one place for a while.

"I'll check in every day." His mouth pressed into a firm line, then he reached out and ran his hand down her arm before threading his fingers through hers. "I'm going to miss you both."

I'm counting on it. "Be careful and don't drive if you're tired."

"I'll be fine." His gaze settled on her mouth and she held her breath.

They stood in view of the ranch hands, her mother and Alex sitting on the porch, eating cookies. Mason watching from the shadows of the barn. *Kiss me, Vic. Give me something to hold on to when you're gone.*

He released her hand, touched a fingertip to the brim of his hat, then climbed into his truck.

Tears burned her eyes as she watched him drive off. The pickup barely stopped at the end of the road before turning onto the highway and speeding south back to Texas.

"WHAT HAPPENED WITH you and my ex-wife?"

The question startled Vic out of his reverie.

"Didn't take Tanya long to figure out you're just like me, did it?"

Vic refused to allow Billings to provoke him into a fight. He had to win today or else he'd slip out of the top ten—but then again maybe that was why Beau was yanking his chain. "My relationship with Tanya is none of your business." He took his gear and walked off, searching for a dark corner to wait for his turn in the chute.

Fat chance. Billings dogged his heels. "Heard that stupid horse she bought came up lame in Fairlie. I bet she ran back to Red Rock to lick her wounds."

Vic put the brakes on and did an about-face. "If you've got nothing nice to say about Tanya, keep your mouth shut. If not, I'll shut it for you." Vic left Billings standing in the cowboy ready area, his jaw hanging like a door missing a hinge.

Vic was glad Tanya had kicked Billings to the curb. He was just sorry she'd been hurt by the jackass. Fairlie had been over a month ago and he'd yet to find the time to visit the farm and check on Alex. And he'd missed Alex's birthday. But Tanya had come through for him and she and her parents had taken Alex to the Denver Zoo and spent the day there. When Vic called to wish him a happy birthday, Alex had been standing in front of the giraffe exhibit. Vic hadn't expected Alex to say anything on the phone and had been surprised when his nephew had told him he liked the mountain goats because they could climb high on the rocks. Then he'd handed the phone back to Tanya.

Later that night Tanya had checked in with Vic and they'd chatted about Alex's day. It had been the first time the boy had visited a zoo, and according to Tanya it was now his most favorite place in the whole world after the horse farm. Vic was grateful Tanya and her folks cared enough to make it a special birthday for Alex, and Vic vowed that when he was finished with rodeo once and for all he'd take Alex to all kinds of places.

The question was not if Vic was ready to walk away from rodeo, but when. He was tired of zigzagging across the country from one state to the next trying to get in as many rodeos as possible. This morning he'd woken in North Dakota and tonight he was competing in Kansas.

He stopped to watch a group of cowboys help one of their friends onto a bronc. He didn't like a crowd around him in the chute. He preferred to go it alone— the path he'd traveled most of his life. But after Tanya and Alex had come into his life, going it alone didn't feel so comfortable anymore.

Vic backed away when the cowboy's name was announced. He closed his eyes and blocked out the noise.

The earthy smell of dirt, cowboy sweat and livestock teased his nose. He willed his muscles to relax, and as soon as they did his spine settled into place. The buzzer sounded and he opened his eyes. His competitor had made it to eight and scored an eighty-one. Beatable.

A bronc named Ring Leader was loaded into the chute. Not until they shut the gate did the animal object to his confinement with a swift kick against the rails. "Good luck with that one." A cowboy guffawed.

The more pissed off the bronc, the better it bucked, the better Vic had a chance of earning a higher score. He shoved his hand into his glove and climbed the rails. He made sure the horse knew he was there before he slid onto its back. Ring Leader stood perfectly still, but Vic wasn't fooled. The horse's hindquarters bunched, the muscles looking as if someone had tucked soccer balls up under his hide.

He adjusted his grip on the rope, knowing that if it wasn't perfect, he could kiss the ride goodbye. Ring Leader didn't give second chances.

"Ladies and gentlemen, turn your attention to chute seven, where seasoned bronc rider Victor Vicario will try to get the best of Ring Leader, a bronc with a history of smashing a cowboy's dream. Vicario needs a win tonight to remain in the top ten."

C'mon, Ring Leader, give me all you've got.

Vic sucked oxygen deep into his lungs, then nodded. As soon as the metal gate swung open, the bronc pounced for freedom. Vic raised his legs and marked out, his spurs rolling front to back in an easy rhythm above the points of the horse's shoulders.

Ring Leader spun hard to the left, but Vic was ready and sank low in the saddle, his core muscles clenched tighter than a slab of cement. The bronc straightened and then pitched forward. Vic's thighs burned with the effort to stay in position. The bronc tried twice more to throw him off his back, but each time Vic outsmarted him. When the buzzer sounded, Ring Leader gave one last buck and Vic held on until he spotted an opening, then launched himself into the air, landing hard on his right shoulder. After so many face-plants during his early years of riding, he'd take a sore shoulder over a broken nose any day.

He rolled to his feet, checked to make sure Ring Leader didn't kick him in the back of the head before he was escorted from the arena, then scooped his hat off the ground, placed it on his head and returned to the cowboy ready area.

He removed his glove, his gaze glued to the score monitor. *Eighty-seven*. He was back in contention.

"Well, folks, it looks like Victor Vicario is on his game today. An eighty-seven puts him in second place behind Joe Peters of Oklahoma. Both cowboys go home with a little jingle in their pockets tonight."

Vic packed his gear and made his way to the rodeo office to pick up his winnings before heading to St. George, Utah. He had to keep pushing himself because every ride was another practice round for the finals in Vegas.

Paycheck in hand he left the arena. As soon as he got behind the wheel of his pickup, he checked his cell phone for messages. *One*. His heart thumped hard as he anticipated hearing Tanya's voice, but the call was from Alex's social worker.

"Victor, this is Renee. We were able to place Alex in a home. They're a nice couple. I think Alex will do well with them. There's only one problem. They can't take him until the middle of January. I certainly understand if you're not able to keep Alex that long. When you have time give me a call and we'll discuss other options. Thanks."

Vic stared out the windshield. He pictured himself dropping Alex off at a strange house in Albuquerque and walking away. He tried to imagine the look on his nephew's face when Vic told him he had to stay at that house and couldn't be with Vic anymore.

Damn it. Vic backed out of the parking spot and turned south instead of west. Forget the rodeo in Utah at the end of the week. He was heading to Albuquerque.

"I DIDN'T KNOW you were in town," Renee said when Vic poked his head around her office door.

"Do you have a few minutes to talk about Alex?"

"Come in." She pointed to the chair across from her desk. "You got my message, then?"

"That's why I'm here."

"If you're worried about the foster family, don't be. The Fieldses are one of the nicest couples I know." She leaned forward, balancing her elbows on the stack of files in front of her. "Richard is a software engineer and Sonja stays at home with the kids during the day."

"Kids?"

"If we place Alex with them, they'll have a total of four foster children living in their home."

"That's a lot."

"They're experienced, responsible parents. The children with them now are ages eight, twelve and fifteen. All girls. Alex would be the only boy."

"Why do the Fieldses want to wait until January to take him?"

"They have a vacation planned and didn't want to take Alex anywhere until they were sure he felt safe and comfortable with them."

The couple sounded perfect.

"Is Alex talking more?"

Vic nodded. "Short sentences. He went to the Denver Zoo for his birthday and Tanya said he loved it."

"I'm glad to hear that. Alex is a sweet boy. With lots of love he's going to be fine."

Love. Would the Fieldses actually love Alex or just care for him? There was a difference. "What's the deal with Natalia?"

"She's doing very well. And she's staying out of trouble."

"Will you eventually give her custody of Alex?"

"Actually Natalia's been cleared to move to Atlanta where a friend found her a factory job with benefits."

"She doesn't want to take Alex with her?"

"No, and we wouldn't let her even if she did. She still has a long way to go before we'd feel confident placing Alex in her care. Right now she doesn't want Alex. We're hoping she'll change her mind after she gets settled in Atlanta and is employed for at least a year there.

If she stays out of trouble, we'll entertain the possibility of reuniting the two." Renee held up her hand. "If Natalia changes her mind and wants Alex with her."

That was never going to happen. Vic doubted his sister would last a month on the new job before she quit. He was embarrassed and pissed off that his sister's life was so screwed up she couldn't care for her own flesh and blood.

"Let me have custody of Alex." When Renee just stared at him, he said, "He's used to me."

"You're a good uncle for wanting to care for your nephew, but I think we can do better by Alex."

"Better? I'm his flesh and blood."

"I'm sorry. That's not what I meant." Renee motioned to Vic's cowboy hat. "Alex can't travel the rodeo circuit with you. I'm aware that many children in this country are homeschooled, but Alex needs socialization with other kids his age. He was locked inside an apartment for four years with no playmates. He needs to be in a school setting."

"What if I stop riding?" A shiver raced down Vic's spine, but he'd gone too far to turn back now. "What if I settle down in one place so Alex can go to school and meet other kids?"

"Where do you plan to live? How do you plan to make a living?"

"Right now the only thing I know for sure is that I won't be living in Albuquerque." For his sake and Alex's they had to keep their distance from the barrio.

"Have you ever done anything other than rodeo?"

"No." Vic's whole life had been dedicated to the

sport, and until Renee had posed the question, he hadn't realized all that he'd given up to ride broncs.

She offered a sympathetic smile. "I appreciate your willingness to help your nephew, but we have to keep in mind what environment will best help Alex learn and grow. The Fieldses are nice people. They'll make sure Alex is available when you're able to visit."

That wasn't good enough. "What if by January I prove that I can provide a stable home for my nephew?"

"Then we'd evaluate all the options before deciding on where to place him."

That left Vic a little over three months to plan out his and Alex's future.

Renee glanced at her watch. "I'm late for a meeting. Stay in touch and let me know how things are going. Next time call before you drop in and I'll introduce you to the Fieldses. I promise you'll like them."

Vic had a lot to think about on the drive to Colorado— he made the seven-hour trip to Longmont in six. It was midnight when he pulled into town and checked himself into a motel. He'd get a few hours of sleep, then call Tanya and tell her he wanted to stop by for a visit.

He tossed his keys on the nightstand, his hat on the chair then collapsed on the bed. He was asleep before he remembered to take off his boots.

TANYA'S CELL PHONE beeped at six in the morning. She fumbled for the phone and when she saw that it was Vic who'd sent her a text message, she sat up and brushed the hair from her eyes.

I'm on my way out to the farm. Invite me for breakfast.

She smiled and texted back. Hot coffee will be waiting. Then she threw back the covers, ran down the hall
to the kitchen and put on a fresh pot of coffee. She took
a quick shower and by the time she'd dressed and returned to the kitchen, Vic's truck was barreling down
the driveway. She slipped her feet into the pair of slip-
pers she kept by the back door, then stepped onto the
porch.

When he got out of the cab and looked her way,
Tanya's heart flipped over. *Play it cool.* He didn't have
to know how badly she'd missed him.

He sauntered up to the house, his eyes never leaving her face. Behind him she noticed her mother and
Mason appear in the barn doorway. When they recognized the visitor, they returned inside the barn, giving
Tanya and Vic a few minutes alone.

"Your hair's wet," Vic said when he reached the
porch steps.

She kept a straight face. "I just got out of the shower."

"Did I wake you?"

"Yes."

His dark gaze roamed over her body and she wondered if he wished she was still in bed and he could
join her. "I've missed you." His gravelly voice drifted
up the steps.

She smiled. "I'm glad."

He chuckled as he climbed the steps. "You would
find pleasure in my misery."

He caressed her cheek, running the pad of his thumb

beneath her eyes. "What's with the dark shadows? Trouble sleeping?"

"I've been worried about you."

His expression softened. "I'm still in one piece."

"Hungry?"

He nodded, but the heat in his stare said food was the last thing on his mind. She took him by the hand and they went inside the house. "Have a seat. Alex won't be up for another hour." She poured two cups of coffee, setting his in front of him and hers on the counter. Then she grabbed the carton of eggs from the fridge and slid a frying pan onto the burner. She didn't ask how he wanted them cooked—she knew. Scrambled. She cracked a half dozen in a bowl then beat them with a fork. While the eggs cooked she pulled out the toaster and dropped two English muffins inside. Then she placed the butter dish and a jar of raspberry preserves on the table before she found the courage to look at him.

If he wasn't going to tell her, then she'd ask. "What are you doing here? Aren't you supposed to be in Oregon? Or wait that was last week. California?" He shook his head. "Texas?" She rolled her eyes. "I can't keep track anymore."

"Minnesota." He sipped his coffee. "I went to see Renee in Albuquerque."

"When?"

"Yesterday."

Tanya stirred the eggs, then remembered Vic liked them spicy, so she fetched the hot sauce from the fridge and put that on the table.

"Don't you want to know why I was in Albuquerque?"

Not really. She was pretty sure it had to do with Alex and she wasn't ready to hear this news. "Why did you go there?"

"They found a foster home for Alex."

Tanya's heart sank.

Chapter Thirteen

They found a home for Alex. When the words finally penetrated Tanya's brain, she forced a smile and said, "That's great."

Vic's sober expression hinted that he didn't agree. "The couple is already fostering three girls. They can't take Alex until January when they return from a vacation they have planned."

Tanya delivered Vic's eggs to the table, then turned back to the counter when the toaster popped up. She added the muffins to his meal then joined him at the table, inhaling her coffee because she desperately needed the jolt of caffeine. They'd both known this day would come sooner or later. "Did you plan to tell Alex today or wait?"

"There's nothing to tell him. I'm not letting him live with the Fieldses."

"What do you mean?"

He shook his head. "I can't do it."

Tanya's pulse raced. "Can't do what?"

"Let Alex go."

Did he mean what she thought he meant? "Spell it out, Vic."

"I want Alex to live with me."

The truth shone in his eyes. Tanya tried to wrap her head around the idea of Vic gaining permanent custody of his nephew and what that meant for his rodeo career. "Did Renee agree to place him with you?" Before Vic had a chance to answer her, Alex strolled into the kitchen, rubbing his eyes. When he noticed his uncle he smiled and hurried across the room. Vic spun on his seat and gave Alex a bear hug.

"Look who's finally out of bed." Vic lifted Alex onto his lap. "I missed you, buddy."

Alex rested his head against his uncle's chest and Tanya had to glance away from the tender scene. Did Vic have any idea what kind of responsibility he was taking on if he agreed to raise Alex? Was he giving up rodeo for good? Where would he and Alex live? Her questions would have to wait because Mason entered the house.

"Looks like my favorite wrangler finally decided to get out of bed."

Mason's voice carried into the kitchen moments before he entered the room, Tanya's mother right behind him. "Hello, Victor," she said.

"Mrs. Coldwater." Vic nodded to Mason. "Sir."

"Jean and Mason will do just fine." Tanya's mother poured a cup of coffee and handed it to Mason. "We didn't know you were coming for a visit." She held out her hand to Alex. "Let Nana Jean find you a pair of wrangling pants so you can help Mason muck the stalls after breakfast."

Alex slid off Vic's lap and slipped his tiny hand into Nana Jean's. When they reached the doorway, Alex pulled free and raced back to Vic. He hugged his uncle, then hurried from the kitchen.

Mason pulled out a chair and sat at the table. "We've enjoyed having Alex stay with us. As you might suspect Nana Jean spoils him."

"I appreciate you helping Tanya look after him." Vic stared Mason in the eye. "As for spoiling my nephew... Alex could use the extra attention after what he's been through."

Tanya assumed Mason had a point to make with Vic or he wouldn't have come into the house. She cleared the dishes from the table and put the food away while she waited for her father to speak his mind.

"You're back in the top ten." Mason slurped his coffee, squinting over the rim of his mug. "Alex told me."

Vic glanced at Tanya.

"Tanya shows Alex the rankings on the computer. Then he reports them to me," Mason said.

"Alex can find your name in the listings," Tanya said. "We've also been practicing our numbers and learning the alphabet by reading lots of books." Then after she tucked Alex in for the night, she'd get back on the computer and view the rodeo rankings again. Now that she understood why winning was so important to Vic, she lived and died each eight seconds with him.

"Tanya says you're from Albuquerque."

Oh boy. Here came the game of twenty questions.

She'd shared some of Vic's situation with Mason and her mother but not all the gory details of his past.

"It's just my sister and Alex in our family now," Vic said.

Mason nodded to Vic's face. "Looks like you tangled with a mean hombre."

Tanya held her breath, wishing Mason hadn't been so blunt. At least she hoped Vic would appreciate that she hadn't blabbed about how he'd gotten the injury.

"Actually it was a family dispute."

"I'm sorry to hear that," Mason said, dropping the subject. "What are your plans after you win that buckle in Vegas?"

There had been no use denying her feelings for Vic when Mason had poked and prodded her for information. Tanya had said every way she knew how without actually speaking the words that she was in love with Vic. Mason was protective of her and she appreciated his concern. He'd warned her that Beau was no good, but she hadn't listened.

Vic's not Beau. Vic was a rodeo cowboy in the sense that he competed in the sport, but that was as far as it went. Vic didn't ride for his ego, fame or fortune. He rode for forgiveness.

"All I know is busting broncs, but I'm a fast learner and I'm not afraid of hard work or a little sweat." Vic nodded at Mason. "I'll find a job doing something."

Mason shoved his chair back. "I better head out to the barn before Raymond has the horses running backwards instead of forward."

Mason and Raymond had developed a love-hate relationship. Raymond listened to Mason's lectures then went off and did his own thing, which most of the time brought about positive results. The only reason Raymond hadn't been let go when Tanya had returned to the farm was she was too busy watching over Alex.

Her mother had offered to babysit so she could spend more time training the horses, but being with Alex made Tanya feel closer to Vic. And sometimes when they were together she imagined the future held more for her and Vic than a goodbye at the end of the road they were traveling down now.

Vic shook Mason's hand. "Thank you for opening your home to my nephew."

"Don't stay away too long or Jean may not give Alex back." Mason set his cup in the sink, kissed Tanya on the cheek and left the house.

"I feel bad," Vic said.

"About what?"

"I never asked you what happened to your real father."

"He was the foreman here at the Red Rock," Jean said, waltzing into the kitchen. Alex climbed onto the chair next to Vic. "We lived in a double-wide in town and Gary commuted to the ranch." She took a box of Cinnamon Cheerios from the cupboard and set it on the table along with a bowl and spoon for Alex. Once she poured the milk, Alex dug in.

"Tanya was in fourth grade." Jean refreshed her coffee and leaned a hip against the counter. "When Mason showed up at the trailer in the middle of the afternoon, I knew something had happened to Gary."

"Dad was repairing a section of fence when he had a heart attack," Tanya said. "He was working alone, so no one knew anything was wrong until he didn't come in for lunch."

"By the time Mason drove out to the pasture and found Gary…it was too late."

"He was young," Vic said.

"Thirty-six," her mother said. "I wasn't working at the time, so Mason offered me a job as his housekeeper and insisted we move the trailer onto his property. And that's how we ended up at Red Rock."

"We lasted about six months in the trailer," Tanya said. "A storm blew through that summer and a tree limb fell onto the trailer, demolishing the kitchen."

"We were only supposed to be in the house temporarily," Jean said. "But Mason talked us into staying longer and we never did move out."

Tanya winked at her mother. "I still remember the morning I walked into the kitchen and caught you and Mason kissing."

"You were fourteen," her mother said. "I guess we couldn't hide our growing affection from you forever."

"I'm glad you married Mason. And I think Dad would approve, too."

"I agree. Your father had a lot of respect for Mason."

Tanya got up from the table and retrieved the bottle of children's vitamins she'd picked up at the drugstore the last time she ran errands in town. She dumped three onto her palm and held them out to Alex. "Pick one." It was a game they played each morning to get Alex to speak. "Batman, Robin or the Joker?"

"Batman."

Alex popped the purple vitamin into his mouth and Tanya moved her hand in front of Vic. "Your turn."

"I'll be Alex's sidekick and take Robin." Vic grinned.

Tanya's mother dropped her gaze from Vic's face. "I'm running errands later." She spoke to Alex. "Do you want to go to the grocery store with me?"

Alex nodded.

"Your nephew's a great helper. He keeps all the food organized in the cart."

"And he knows if he goes with Nana Jean he gets a treat at the checkout." Tanya winked at Alex.

"Will you be here when we return, Victor?"

"No. I need to get back on the road."

"Then I guess we'll see you the next time you come through town."

After her mother left the kitchen, Tanya set the empty cereal bowl in the sink and loaded the dishwasher while Vic and Alex chatted.

"I'm glad you're being a good boy for Tanya and her folks," Vic said. "Do you like living here?"

Tanya peeked over her shoulder and saw Alex nod.

"Do you think you'd mind staying here with Tanya awhile longer? I have a few more broncs I need to ride."

Another nod.

"There's something important I want to ask you." Vic scooted his chair closer to Alex. "That nice lady named Renee is trying to find you a new family to live with."

Alex dropped his gaze.

"But I was thinking that I'd really like you to live with me after I finish rodeoing."

Alex lifted his head, his eyes wide.

"Would you like us to be a family?" Vic asked.

"Yes." The word came out loud and clear.

"I was hoping you'd say that." Vic hugged Alex. "We'll talk about it more the next time I visit."

Alex ran from the room.

"Are you sure that was smart to do?" she asked.

"What do you mean?"

"Promising that Alex can live with you when nothing for sure has been decided?"

"I'm his uncle. They're not going to deny me custody."

Her mouth dropped open. "What if you don't win a national title in December?" Good grief, Tanya didn't want to jinx Vic, but he could get injured or just have an off day in the arena and not win. And what about his promise to Cruz? "What if you don't win a buckle this year?" What would he do with Alex if he returned to the circuit next year?

"I'm not losing this year." He got up from the table. "I've got all the motivation I need to win." He pressed a soft kiss to her mouth. "I need to win for Cruz so I can make peace with the past and I need to win for Alex so we can be a family. I'm not going to let him grow up in foster care."

Was he going to win so *they* had a future together?

"Where will you live? What about a job?" *What about me?*

He pressed his finger against her lips. "I don't have all the answers yet, but I will. There's just one thing I need to know before I leave today."

"What's that?"

"Will you still be around when I'm done with rodeo?"

"What are you asking, Vic?"

"I'm asking you to wait for me."

Then tell me what I mean to you—don't make me guess.

He backed away from her. "Alex and I need you." He walked to the door, then stopped and turned. "I want both of you in my life. That's plenty of incentive for me to win."

Tanya stared at the empty doorway, her heart swelling with hope and fear. Vic hadn't said he loved her—he'd said he needed her. There was a difference.

"Where are you?"

Tanya's voice drifted into Vic's car and he pressed his cell phone harder against the side of his head. "At the Best Western in Ventura." It was the second Saturday in November and he'd just taken third place in his final rodeo of the regular season in California. The next time he climbed onto a bronc, he'd be in Vegas the first week in December.

"Congrats on third place," she said.

"They posted the scores already?" He'd stopped for a bite to eat. Then as soon as he'd keyed into his room, he called Tanya. He hadn't had a chance to check the standings. "Where did I end up?"

"Ninth."

Good enough to make it to the finals. "Who kicked me out of eight place?"

"Yanger moved up after his win in Idaho," Tanya

said. "Why don't you rest here at Red Rock before you go to Vegas? Alex misses you."

"Is he the only one who misses me?" He heard Tanya's soft sigh and closed his eyes, imagining her lying in bed, a naked thigh resting on top of the sheet. Her T-shirt clinging to her breasts.

"I miss you, Vic."

"I miss you, too." *More than I expected to. More than you'll ever know.* Traveling alone after having Tanya and Alex tag along with him this past summer didn't feel right anymore. The life of solitude he'd been comfortable with for so long now suffocated him. "I've got to get some things figured out before the finals."

"What things?"

"Just…stuff." Like where he was going to live with Alex and how he could support them. He wanted a plan for the future because when he asked Tanya if she'd share it with him and Alex, he didn't want to give her any reason to turn him down.

"At least spend Thanksgiving Day at the farm with us," she said. "I can't stand the thought of you sitting in a motel room eating fast food by yourself."

"I won't be alone. I'll be at the Juan Alvarez Ranch for Boys northwest of Albuquerque." It was a lie. He was planning to visit Riley and Maria the week after Thanksgiving—right before the National Finals Rodeo in Vegas. "My former high school teacher and her husband run the ranch for trouble teens. They helped me get on the right path." *Until I screwed up and derailed Cruz.*

"Oh."

Vic winced at the hurt in Tanya's voice. *Don't give up on me, babe.* "How's Alex?"

"Good. He's talking a lot more. His therapist said she thinks it would really help his social skills if he enrolled in a preschool program after Christmas."

"Sounds like a plan." And another reason he had to win next month. "Renee called a few days ago. I told her I hadn't changed my mind. I still intend to seek custody of Alex."

"And…?"

"She's on my side and hopes the judge rules in my favor."

"Vic…what happens if you don't win in Vegas?"

"I'm not going to lose, Tanya. I promise." He had too much riding on the line. "I gotta go. I'll call Alex on Thanksgiving. Tell him I miss him." He disconnected the call before he changed his mind and decided to spend the holiday at Red Rock.

The next time he saw Tanya, he wanted to be able to tell her that he loved her. That he wanted a future with her and Alex. That he wanted the three of them to be a family. And he couldn't do that until he had more to offer them than just himself.

"THIS IS A SURPRISE," Riley Fitzgerald said as he descended the porch steps of his ranch house. He shook hands with Vic. "It's been almost a year since you showed your face around here." He pointed to the house. "Maria's in town shopping."

"I just spoke with her on the phone. She said the ranch hands had taken all the boys to a carnival." Vic's gaze skipped over the buildings and the corrals where several horses grazed.

"Is that why you decided to stop here?" Riley asked. "Because Cruz is gone?"

Vic wouldn't lie to his mentor. "Yes."

"For both your sakes you two need to talk."

"We'll talk…eventually."

"You've been saying that for years. When is it going to be the right time?"

"Next month."

"Next month is in three days."

Vic didn't need a reminder. "After the NFR."

"This is your fourth time, isn't it?"

"Fourth and last."

"What do you mean by that?"

"Whether I win or lose I'm hanging up my spurs for good."

"How'd you come to that decision?"

"I'm fighting for custody of my nephew."

"Maria and Judge Hamel talk often, so I probably know more than I should. I'm sorry about your mother."

Vic nodded. He didn't want discuss his mom's death or sister's move to Atlanta. "I need your help."

"Anything."

"Will you watch me ride and give me some pointers?"

"Vic, you're damn good at busting broncs. You don't need advice from me."

"Everything's got to be perfect this time. There's no room for error."

"C'mon on. We've got a bucker that I don't let the boys get on."

Vic followed Riley across the yard.

"Cruz and I ride him once in a while when we get to thinking we're younger than we really are."

"My right knee's been bothering me," Vic confessed. He'd landed awkwardly in Ventura and had limped out of the arena, worried he was finished for the season. He'd driven to the nearest ER to have his knee checked, but nothing was torn. He'd strained the ligaments but the doc had claimed there were already signs of arthritis in the knee joint.

"Does spurring hurt?" Riley asked.

"A little." Riley raised his eyebrow and Vic said. "More than a little, but not enough to keep me from riding."

They entered the barn and went into the tack room. "You need to protect your knee before you ride." Riley confiscated a roll of elastic bandage they kept on hand for the horses and wrapped Vic's knee tight enough to support the joint.

"Before I bring out Earthquake, let's use one of the horses we let the boys play cowboy on. You'll be able to try a few different techniques without getting thrown."

"Sure."

Riley led a horse from his stall. "This is Spitfire. He retired from the circuit ten years ago, but he's still got a little gas left in him." Vic admired his mentor for buying former rodeo horses that hadn't been good enough to use for breeding. Not only teenagers, but old broncs got a second chance at the ranch.

"I have an idea that might take the pressure off your knee." Riley backed Spitfire into the chute, then straddled the horse. "Does the inside or outside of your knee hurt when you mark out?"

"The inside."

"Okay, slide down a little farther than you normally do in the saddle and shift your weight slightly to the left so you're not centered over the horse's neck."

"That's risky if the bronc twists left coming out of the chute," Vic said.

"It is, but I think you have the strength in your core to keep yourself upright. When you spur in this position, it should take some of the pressure off the knee joint." Riley hopped off the horse. "Give it a try."

Vic gave it more than a try. After three times on Spitfire, Vic rode Earthquake. An hour later he decided he'd had enough practice. Riley's suggestion had worked and with a few minor adjustments, Vic knew exactly how to keep his body in position. All that remained for him to do was show up at the NFR and ride.

"Thanks for your help," Vic said.

"Maria and I are bringing the boys to Vegas to watch you," Riley said.

"It'll be nice to have a few friends in the crowd."

"You'll have more than a few friends. Most of the kids at the ranch are coming, too. We're chartering a bus."

Even more pressure to win.

Riley grasped his arm. "Whether you win or lose, Vic, you've had a hell of a run."

"Tell Maria I said hello."

"Stick around. She should be back soon."

"I better get on the road." Vic didn't want to chance running into Cruz.

"On second thought, you probably should." Riley smiled. "Maria's miffed that she had to find out from Judge Hamel that your nephew is staying with the Coldwaters up in Longmont."

"It's a long story."

Riley chuckled. "All three of you cowboys of the Rio Grande have long stories."

"You hear much from Alonso?" Maria had told Vic that his friend had married and he and his wife had a baby girl in July.

"Alonso and Hannah are joining us in Vegas. Hannah's brother, Luke, has his sights set on rodeoing after high school. Alonso told him about you and Luke's looking forward to watching you ride."

"Tanya's bringing Alex to Vegas so you and Maria will meet them there."

"Does this Tanya McGee have anything to do with you wanting to raise your nephew?"

"Maybe."

"Where did you two meet?"

"On the circuit. She's a barrel racer when she isn't training horses for her stepfather."

"What are your plans after rodeo?"

"Find a place to settle down and look for work."

"I can always use another mentor for the kids." Riley opened his arms wide. "There's plenty of room for you to build a home on the property."

Vic swallowed twice before he found his voice. "I

appreciate all you and Maria have done for me through the years. Without your support…" He shook his head. "I'll give it some thought."

Riley grasped Vic's shoulder and squeezed. "No matter what the future holds for you, Maria and I will always be your family. You can count on us to be there for you."

Vic had been able to count on very few people in his life and Riley's words meant the world to him. If he could be half the man Riley was, Alex should consider himself lucky to have Vic as an uncle and a father. "See you in Vegas."

Vic glanced in the rearview when he drove away. As Riley's figure grew smaller and smaller, Vic's determination grew stronger and stronger. No matter what happened in Vegas, he had a lot to look forward to the rest of his life and it was time to move on. He'd give it one last shot for Cruz and hope in the end that what he had to offer his friend was more than an apology.

Chapter Fourteen

"Mr. Vicario?"

Vic stopped twenty feet inside the entrance to the Thomas and Mack Center in Las Vegas, Nevada, late Saturday afternoon and searched for the feminine voice in the milling crowd of rodeo fans. A petite blonde appeared in front of him. She flashed a tentative smile.

"The saddle-bronc contestants have been signing autographs for the past hour. There's still time to join them if you'd like. The tables are located across from the west entrance on the ground level."

"No, thanks." He stepped past the young woman and headed for the cowboy ready area. He hadn't signed autographs once in all the years he'd competed, and he wasn't about to make an exception today. He didn't care to be in the limelight. The final day of competition wasn't about him—it had never been about him.

The final go-round had always been about Cruz and making amends.

He turned the corner, leaving the crowds behind and stopped at the sign-in table to pick up his number. Then as he'd done the previous nights, he disappeared into the shadows beneath the stands. He'd gotten good at hiding from the fans and media, and the out-of-the-way space suited him and his twisted nerves just fine.

He propped his back against the cement wall and closed his eyes—the steak and potato he'd eaten three hours ago sat in his stomach like a brick.

He reached into his pocket, his fingers squeezing his cell phone. He'd spoken to Tanya and Alex a few hours earlier while he sat in his motel room—a janky dive off the strip where no one would expect an NFR rodeo cowboy to stay. The sound of Alex's high-pitched voice saying, "I hope you win, Uncle Vic," echoed through his mind. The therapist Tanya found had made great strides with Alex and he was talking all the time now, asking a million questions about rodeo, which Tanya said Mason was more than happy to answer.

Tanya and her folks were staying at a hotel on the strip and had been present every night he'd competed. He'd limited his contact with them—a quick meal after his win before returning to his room—because each time he looked into Tanya's eyes he lost a little bit of his will to win. He wanted this over with so he could move on with his life. His whole world had been rodeo for so long that when Tanya and Alex had wiggled their way into his heart, they'd opened his eyes to the possibility of a future where he could be at peace with the past.

Tonight was the beginning of tomorrow and every day after with Tanya and Alex. No matter what happened in the arena, this was his final ride. He'd failed Cruz all those years ago, but Alex coming into Vic's

life had given him a new purpose, and that was raising his nephew.

Tonight he was going up against Kenny Higgins.
The twenty-one-year-old Irish kid had come out of nowhere this past July and had made a name for himself.
His spirited personality matched his red hair and he'd
become a crowd favorite. One of them would walk away
with the championship buckle. Vic hoped it was him,
but no matter the outcome he'd have no regrets when
he took his last walk through the cowboy ready area.

Images flashed through his mind at warp speed; him,
Cruz and Alonso running the streets of Albuquerque.
Ducking behind Dumpsters to avoid the police patrol-
ling their neighborhood. Cruz and Alonso waiting for
him when he left the emergency room after he'd received fifty-seven stitches in his face.

Cruz grabbing the gun from his hand.

Cruz sitting in the back of the patrol car.

Cruz being sentenced to prison.

And Vic being sentenced to a rodeo career he'd never
wanted. He recalled his first official rodeo where he'd
broken his wrist after being tossed by a bronc named
Ugly. The second rodeo, the third, the fifteenth…when
he'd finally made it to the buzzer. Driving down a de-
serted stretch of highway to the next event. Sleeping in
the backseat of his pickup. His first trophy. First check.
First visit to the finals in Vegas…second…third. Tanya
stranded on the side of the road in the rain. Her smile.
The feel of her soft skin beneath his hands. Alex waving
goodbye. Tanya's worried gaze staring after his pickup.

Vic felt it coming…the slow clenching of his intestines, his chest compressing, his mouth watering… He turned his head and puked. Not once but three times until there was nothing left in his gut.

"You better drink this."

The back of Vic's hand froze against his mouth. His sour stomach forgotten, he straightened. A can of soda appeared in front of his eyes. With shaking fingers he accepted the drink. He swished the carbonated beverage around his mouth, then spat it out before chugging several swallows.

Then he turned and faced his past.

"You look like someone pulled you through a knothole backward."

Vic hadn't seen or spoken to Cruz all week, but Tanya had mentioned that Cruz and Alonso and their families had arrived the night of his first ride. She'd asked if he'd wanted to visit with them, but he couldn't face any of them until he ridden his last bronc.

He studied Cruz's chiseled face—searching for the teenager he'd hung out with years ago, but there wasn't a hint of boy left in his face or body. His dark brown eyes were guarded. Cruz wasn't the same homey he'd run wild with in the barrio. Neither was Vic.

"You gonna say something or just stand there looking at me like I'm a ghost?" Cruz asked.

"Sorry." The apology slipped from Vic's lips and he winced.

"We can start there. It's as good a place as any."

"I should have listened to you that night and not met up with the Los Locos." Vic dropped his gaze. "But I was determined to make things right for my sister."

"Maria told me what happened to Camila. I'm sorry."

"It was all for nothing. Camila took her own life and the baby inside her and you got sent to prison." Vic poked himself in the chest. "It should have been me serving time, not you."

"I think my sentence might have been easier than yours."

"That's a stupid thing to say."

Cruz spread his arms wide. "What the hell are you doing, man?"

"Isn't it obvious? I'm trying to win a buckle."

"If I recall, you hated rodeo." Cruz chuckled. "I remember when Riley talked you into getting on the back of Make Believe. Remember that ornery horse with one ear?"

Vic smiled at the memory.

"Damn, that horse had a mean kick. You flew right over its neck and landed on your face. Blood spewed from your nose and you cussed up a storm, swearing you'd rather get shot on the streets than bust another bronc."

If Vic could go back in time, he'd sure in hell make different choices.

"You've dedicated your life to something you hate. Why?"

"Rodeo has grown on me." There was some truth in the statement. Vic had developed a thirst for the adrenaline rush he experienced when he straddled a bronc, and he liked pitting himself against a wild horse, testing his skills. But he'd never lived or died by his next ride like most rodeo cowboys.

"You threw away a lot of years."

"No more than you were forced to behind bars." Vic struggled to keep his voice even. "I stole your future from you."

Cruz's eyes widened. "You're not saying what I think you're saying, are you?"

"I've been trying to win you a buckle…the buckle you would have earned yourself if you'd had the chance."

"Damn it, Vic." Cruz whipped off his hat and ran his fingers through his hair. "You can't know that I would have won a championship if I'd had a rodeo career. Hell, who's to say I would even have stuck it out after the first year?"

"Don't patronize me." Vic jabbed his finger in the air. "You wanted a buckle and you were gonna be good enough to win one. Riley said he'd never seen a guy with your natural talent. You had NFR champion written all over you, Cruz."

"So you think if you win the buckle tonight, everything will be square between us?"

The blood drained from Vic's face. "I don't know. Will it?"

"If you're looking for forgiveness, Vic, just ask for it."

That was too easy. "I thought a buckle—"

"A buckle isn't going to make all those years in prison disappear. I'll be honest with you. I was angry for a long time after I went away."

It took more courage to look Cruz in the eye than it ever had to ride a mean bronc.

"But I've made peace with the past." Cruz's mouth drew down. "But I see now that I wasn't alone serving my sentence behind bars. You were right there with me every day."

"I didn't know how else to make it up to you," Vic said. "I don't have anything to give you."

"What about your friendship?"

"How can you want to be friends with me after what happened to you?"

"Life works in weird ways. I met Sara and she helped me through some pretty dark times when I got out on parole." He smiled. "There's nothing like the love of a good woman to show you what's really important in life."

That was the truth.

"We'd both do well to let go of the past. Better memories are in front of us, not behind us."

"I'm going to take your advice after tonight."

"Good. Maybe now Maria will quit worrying about her three amigos."

Vic chuckled. "I can't believe I've devoted my life to chasing a buckle that neither one of us gives a crap about."

"That's a hell of a confidence booster before the final ride of your career." Cruz grinned. Then his expression sobered. "I don't look back often anymore, but when I do, I see now that you had it a lot worse than me and Alonso. We all had crappy home lives, but you're the only one of us who had to carry his childhood scars on his face for the whole world to see."

Vic rubbed the puckered flesh.

"I think we've both suffered enough."

Vic couldn't agree more, but it wasn't easy to let go of the guilt.

"What about Alex?" Cruz asked.

"What about him?"

"Maria told me you're seeking custody of your nephew."

"If I want to keep him I have to settle in one place and find permanent employment."

"There's room for you and Alex at the boys' ranch."

"Maybe." Vic appreciated Cruz's blessing to live where he and his wife had put down roots, but Vic wasn't making any decisions until he knew where he stood with Tanya. If he didn't win, all Vic had to offer his friend was his humble apology.

"If it's your last go-around, then I hope you're riding for the right reason."

"What do you mean?"

"I've already forgiven you, Vic. If you need to win today, then win for Alex so you can give him the life that you and I never had as kids. And win for *you* so you can finally forgive yourself."

"How can I not win after that speech?"

"You better. Everyone, including Judge Hamel, is sitting in the stands watching." Cruz tipped his hat. "Break a leg, dumb-ass."

Vic grinned. *Dumb-ass* had been Cruz's favorite name to call someone when they were teenagers. They weren't teenagers anymore and if Cruz was willing to let bygones be bygones, Vic had to respect that. For twelve years he'd been torn up inside over what had happened to his friend, and it had only taken a five-minute conversation with Cruz for the burden of guilt to be lifted from his shoulders.

Vic closed his eyes and willed his body to relax. The culmination of years of hard work and dedication was eight seconds away. He left his hiding place and stood with the other cowboys near the chutes. Then he searched the stands for his fan club. He spotted Tanya first—her auburn hair shining among a mass of muted colors. Alex sat next to her, listening to the Fitzgerald twins chatter in his ear. Farther down the row sat Tanya's parents with Riley and Maria. A pretty blonde with a brown-haired little girl in her lap sat next to Cruz, and at the end of the row Alonso held a pink-wrapped bundle against his shoulder, his wife and her teenage brother by his side. Vic's extended family. While he'd been chasing his demons to hell and back across the United States, the people who meant the most to him had shown up tonight—for him. And not because they expected him to win a buckle.

Vic's path in life had led him to this moment—a rebirth. His final ride was an eight-second baptism—the death and burial of his past and the birth of his future and new life.

"Ladies and gentlemen, welcome to the final round of the saddle-bronc competition here at the Thomas and Mack Center in lucky Las Vegas!"

Vic willed Tanya to look his way. She must have heard his heart call out to her, because their gazes connected. She whispered in Alex's ear, and he looked Vic's way. Vic raised a hand, acknowledging that he saw them, then placed his palm against his heart. Tanya pressed her fingers to her mouth and blew him a kiss. No matter who came out the winner tonight—him or the bronc—Vic wasn't leaving the arena until he proposed to Tanya. He didn't have a ring. He didn't have much of a plan. He just had his heart to give to her as a down payment on their life together—if she'd have him.

He turned away, needing to clear his head of her image and focus on the present. He buckled his spurs and pulled on his riding glove.

"This is do-or-die time for these cowboys, and we've seen some spectacular rides during this event. One cowboy in particular has blown up the score clock this week." The crowd quieted as they listened to the announcer's spiel. "Victor Vicario from Albuquerque, New Mexico, is a rodeo veteran who's had a lot of success the past few years. This is his fourth appearance at the NFR." Applause thundered through the crowd.

"Vicario has placed either first or second each time out of the gate this week. He and Kenny Higgins from Jackson Hole, Wyoming, are neck and neck in the race for the buckle tonight.

"Up first is Vicario. This cowboy will be strutting his stuff on Cyclone, a two-time world champion bronc from the Kyle J. Reed Ranch south of Tulsa, Oklahoma." Images of the bronc flashed across the Jumbotron, and music blared through the loudspeakers. When the noise died down, the announcer finished his commentary. "Cyclone spins like a tornado. Let's see if Vicario has the stamina to go all the way on this bronc."

Vic closed his ears to the noise and flexed his sore

knee. He wore an elastic bandage beneath his jeans, but after a week of tough rides, the joint ached like hell. He turned his thoughts inward, reminding himself to lean left as he came out of the chute to help keep the pressure off his knee. A rodeo helper called his name and he opened his eyes.

He sucked in a deep breath and climbed the rails, then eased onto Cyclone's back. The bronc behaved—he'd been to this show before and wasn't wasting his energy in the chute—he'd save his wild side for when he broke free from his confinement. Vic threaded the rope through his fingers, aware of a subtle difference in the tenseness of his muscles. The adrenaline pumping through his body felt different for this ride—euphoric. Instead of the normal anxiety gripping his gut, there was an eagerness to meet this final challenge head-on.

With his love for Tanya and Alex tucked away inside his heart, he nodded to the gateman.

Cyclone shot into the arena, then delivered a series of explosive kicks, challenging Vic like never before. Riley Fitzgerald's voice echoed inside Vic's head.

Lean sideways.

A little more.

There you go.

Watch the knee.

Turn your ankle in when you spur.

That's it.

He's coming out of the spin.

Balance.

Watch your right shoulder, it's too high.

Keep that left arm in the air.

You got this.
He's tiring.
Finish strong!

After years of going it alone and miles and miles of highway paved with guilt, Vic was nearing the finish line. When the buzzer sounded, he double-downed, finding renewed strength as he waited for an opening to dismount. There it was. He threw himself off Cyclone, hitting the ground hard. He rolled to his feet and scrambled to safety. When the rodeo helpers had control of Cyclone, Vic picked his hat up and stood there, his boot heels sinking in the dirt as rodeo fans came to their feet and applauded, the noise deafening.

Buckle or no buckle, this was a hell of a sendoff. He waved to the crowd, then walked out of the arena for the last time. Nothing to do now but wait to see what Higgins did on his bronc.

When he entered the cowboy ready area, his competitors offered their congratulations and then shifted their attention to the score clock, waiting to see what the judges thought of Vic's ride.

No matter what number flashed across the Jumbotron, Vic's journey was at an end and he was at peace.

"Ninety-two!" the announcer shouted. The fans erupted in a frenzy, chanting his name. Vic had landed his highest score of the week on Cyclone.

"Higgins has got his work cut out for him!" The announcer waited for the noise to die down. "This cowboy will need a darn near perfect ride on The Devil's Due, a veteran bronc known for stealing dreams."

Vic removed his spurs and riding glove and stuffed

them into his gear bag. He didn't care to watch Higgins's ride. He needed to see Tanya. He didn't have to go far to find her and Alex. They were waiting for him right outside the cowboy ready area.

As soon as Alex saw Vic, he smiled and raced toward his uncle. Vic dropped his gear bag and crouched down, ignoring the sharp pain in his knee. His nephew's little body slammed into Vic's chest and he hugged the boy close.

"Hey, little man. I missed you." Vic glanced up as Tanya approached, her eyes shining with tears.

"Nothing like showing off for your last ride, cowboy," she said.

He grinned, not giving a damn how it contorted his mouth. Alex patted Vic's chest and didn't stop until Vic gave him his full attention. "What is it?"

"Can you come home?"

Hearing Alex speak out loud only convinced Vic he was doing the right thing by walking away from rodeo. "Yeah, buddy. I'm coming home for good now." *Home*. No four-letter word had ever sounded so good. He stood up and held out his hand to Tanya. She stepped into his embrace and he buried his face in her neck. "I love you, Tanya."

Tanya clutched fistfuls of his shirt. "I love you, too, Vic. So much."

"I'm giving you fair warning right here...right now. We're getting married."

She brushed her mouth against his. "I'm going to hold you to that promise, cowboy." Her shimmering gaze told him without words that she wanted to spend the rest of her life with him and Alex.

"We have a lot to talk about," he said.

Before either one of them had a chance to say another word, the buzzer sounded and the crowd went crazy. Higgins had made it to eight. Vic and Tanya ignored the commotion, their attention focused on each other.

"I've already spoken to Mason," Tanya said. "It was his idea."

"What idea?"

"Mason could use an extra ranch hand. Do you think you could be happy at Red Rock?"

"I could be happy anywhere you are, Tanya." If Vic rode fence the rest of his life, he'd be content as long as Tanya and Alex were happy. He'd seen enough of this great country to last him a lifetime, and he was more than ready to set down roots and call Longmont, Colorado, home.

"Mason said he'd give us ten acres to build a house of our own on."

"You were pretty sure I was going to propose to you," he said.

"Actually I was pretty sure I was going to propose to you." She smiled. "But you beat me to the punch."

"And you're okay with…" He dropped his gaze to his nephew.

Tanya drew Alex into their circle. "We've been a family since July and we're going to stay one."

Vic's throat swelled shut and he couldn't have spoken if he'd tried. So he kissed Tanya, blocking out the noisy fans. He savored her sweet lips and the near perfect future that awaited them as soon as they left the Thomas and Mack Center.

"Ladies and gentlemen, Higgins's score fell a few points short and this year's national champion saddle-bronc cowboy is Victor Vicario!"

"You did it," Tanya whispered against his mouth.

When the kiss ended, Vic glanced up and spotted Cruz and Alonso waiting to congratulate him. Tanya took Alex's hand and walked off to join her parents and the rest of Vic's fan club.

Vic, Alonso and Cruz stood together, each trading looks of forgiveness. Then Cruz spoke. "Now that we've taken care of all that bullshit, it's time the three of us had a beer together."

"Amen," Alonso said, clasping Vic's shoulder. "Go get your buckle, so we can get out of here and celebrate."

"Cruz's buckle," Vic corrected Alonso.

Cruz snorted. "Are you kidding me? I could have ridden Cyclone backward with a blindfold on and gotten a higher score."

"Oh, you could, huh?" Vic punched Cruz playfully in the arm. "I'll tell you what. You do the riding next season, because I'm done."

"Guess we'll see what the next generation does on the circuit," Alonso said, his gaze sliding to his brother-in-law.

"Maybe we should make a wager right now." Cruz nodded at his daughter. "I'm betting Dani is the first female bull rider to win the NFR."

Alonso whistled between his teeth. "I'll wager my

brother-in-law, Luke, wins more than one national championship buckle."

Vic's gaze swung to his nephew, and his chest tightened when Alex smiled at him. "And I bet my nephew, Alex, is smarter than all the rest of us and stays away from rodeo."

The three friends busted up laughing and joined the others. Vic swung Alex onto his shoulders and took Tanya's hand. "After I talk to the media, we'll make wedding plans."

"There's no rush." Tanya's smile wrapped Vic in its warmth. "While we're making plans for the rest of our life, we'll just start living it."

* * * * *

Read on for a sneak preview
of ONCE A RANCHER by
#1 New York Times *bestselling author*
Linda Lael Miller,
the first title in her brand-new series,
THE CARSONS OF MUSTANG CREEK.

CHAPTER ONE

SLATER CARSON WAS bone-tired, as he was after every film wrapped, but it was the best kind of fatigue—part pride and satisfaction in a job well done, part relief, part "bring it," that anticipatory quiver in the pit of his stomach that would lead him to the next project, and the one after that.

This latest film had been set in a particularly remote area, emphasizing how the Homestead Act had impacted the development of not just the American West, but the country as a whole. It had been his most ambitious effort to date. The sheer scope was truly epic, and as he watched the uncut footage on his computer monitor, he *knew*.

160 Acres was going to touch a nerve.

Yep. This one would definitely hit home with the viewers, new and old.

His previous effort, a miniseries on the Lincoln County War in New Mexico, had won prizes and garnered great reviews, and he'd sold the rights to one of the media giants for a shitload of money. Like *Lincoln County*, *160 Acres* was good, solid work. The researchers, camera operators and other professionals he worked with were the top people in the business, as committed to the films as he was.

And that was saying something.

No doubt about it, the team had done a stellar job the last time around, but this—well, *this* was the best yet. A virtual work of art, if he did say so himself.

"Boss?"

Slater leaned back in his desk chair and clicked the pause button. "Hey, Nate," he greeted his friend and personal assistant. "What do you need?"

Like Slater, Nate Wheaton had just gotten back from the film site, where he'd taken care of a thousand details, and it was a safe bet that the man was every bit as tired as he looked. Short, blond, energetic and not more than twenty years old, Nate was a dynamo; the production had come together almost seamlessly, in large part because of his talent, persistence and steel-trap brain.

"Um," Nate murmured, visibly unplugging, shifting gears. He was moving into off-duty mode, and God knew, he'd earned it. "There's someone to see you." He inclined his head in the direction of the outer office, rubbed the back of his neck and let out an exasperated sigh. "The lady insists she needs to talk to you and only you. I tried to get her to make an appointment, but she says it has to be now."

Slater suppressed a sigh of his own. "It's ten o'clock at night."

"I've actually pointed that out," Nate said, glancing at his phone. "It's five *after*, to be exact." Like Slater himself, Nate believed in exactness, which was at once a blessing and a curse. "She claims it can't possibly wait until morning, whatever 'it' is. But if I hadn't been walking into the kitchen I wouldn't have heard the knock."

"How'd she even find me?" The crew had flown in late, driven out to the vineyard/ranch, and Slater had figured that no one, other than his family, knew he was in town. Or out of town. Whatever qualified as far as the ranch was concerned.

Nate looked glumly resigned. "I have no idea. She refused to say. I'm going to bed. If you need anything else, come and wake me, but bring a sledgehammer, because I'd probably sleep through anything less." A pause, another sigh, deeper and wearier than the last. "That was quite the shoot."

The understatement of the day.

Slater drew on the last dregs of his energy, shoved a hand through his hair and said, "Well, point her in this direction, if you don't mind, and then get yourself some shut-eye."

He supposed he sounded normal, but on the inside, he was drained. He'd given everything he had to *160 Acres*, and then some, and there was no hope of charging his batteries. He'd blown through the last of his physical resources hours ago.

Resentment at the intrusion nibbled at his famous equanimity; he was used to dealing with problems on the job—ranging from pesky all the way to apocalyptic—but at home, damn it, he expected to be left alone. He needed rest, downtime, a chance to regroup, and home was where he did those things.

One of his younger brothers ran the Carson ranch,

and the other managed the vineyard and winery. The arrangement worked out pretty well. Everyone had his own role to play, and the sprawling mansion was big enough even for three competitive males to live in relative peace. Especially since Slater was gone half the time anyway.

"Will do." Nate left the study, and a few minutes later the door opened.

Before Slater could make the mental leap from one moment to the next, a woman—quite possibly the most beautiful woman he'd ever seen—stormed across the threshold, dragging a teenage boy by the arm.

She was a redhead, with the kind of body that would resurrect a dead man, let alone a tired one.

And Slater had a fondness for redheads; he'd dated a lot of them over the years. This one was all sizzle, and her riot of coppery curls, bouncing around her straight, indignant shoulders, seemed to blaze in the dim light.

It took him a moment, but he finally recovered enough to clamber to his feet and say, "I'm Slater Carson. Can I help you?"

This visitor, whoever she was, had his full attention. Fascinating.

The redhead poked the kid, who was taller than she was by at least six inches, and she did it none too gently. The boy flinched; he was lanky, clad in a Seahawks T-shirt, baggy jeans and half-laced shoes. He looked bewildered, ready to bolt.

"Start talking, buster," the redhead ordered, glowering up at the kid. "And no excuses." She shook her head. "I'm being nice here," she said when the teenager didn't speak. "Your father would kick you into the next county."

Just his luck, Slater thought, with a strange, nostalgic detachment. She was married.

While he waited for the next development, he let his gaze trail over the goddess, over a sundress with thin straps on shapely shoulders, a midthigh skirt and a lot of silky, pale skin. She was one of the rare titian types who didn't have freckles, although Slater wouldn't be opposed to finding out if there might be a few tucked out of sight. White sandals with a small heel finished off the look, and all that glorious hair was loose and flowing down her back.

The kid, probably around fourteen, cleared his throat. He stepped forward and laid one of the magnetic panels from the company's production truck on the desk.

Slater, caught up in the unfolding drama, hadn't noticed the sign until then.

Interesting.

"I'm sorry," the boy gulped out, looking miserable and, at the same time, a little defiant. "I took this." He glanced briefly at the woman beside him, visibly considered giving her some lip, and just as visibly reconsidered. Smart kid. "I thought it was pretty cool," he explained, all knees and elbows and youthful angst. Color climbed his neck and burned in his face. "I know it was wrong, okay? Stealing is stealing, and my stepmother's ready to cuff me and haul me off to jail, so if that's what you want, too, mister, go for it."

Stepmother?

Slater was still rather dazed, as though he'd stepped

off a wild carnival ride before it was through its whole
slew of loop de loops.

"His father and I are divorced." She said it curtly,
evidently reading Slater's expression.

Well, Slater reflected, that was good news. She did
look young to be the kid's mother. And now that he
thought about it, the boy didn't resemble her in the
slightest, with his dark hair and eyes.

Finally catching up, he raised his brows, feeling a
flicker of something he couldn't quite identify, along
with a flash of sympathy for the boy. He guessed the
redhead was in her early thirties. While she seemed to
be in charge of the situation, Slater suspected she might
be in over her head. Clearly, the kid was a handful.

It was time, Slater decided, still distanced from himself, to speak up.

"I appreciate your bringing it back," he managed,
holding the boy's gaze but well aware of the woman
on the periphery of his vision. "These aren't cheap."

Some of the F-you drained out of the kid's expression. "Like I said, I'm sorry. I shouldn't have done it."

"You made a mistake," Slater agreed quietly. "We've
all done things we shouldn't have at one time or another. You did what you could to make it right, and
that's good." He paused. "Life's all about the choices
we make, son. Next time, try to do better." He felt a grin
lurking at one corner of his mouth. "I would've been
really ticked off if I had to replace this."

The boy looked confused. "Why? You're rich."

Slater had encountered that reasoning before—over
the entire course of his life, actually. His family *was*

wealthy, and had been for well over a century. They ran cattle, owned vast stretches of Wyoming grassland, and now, thanks to his mother's roots in the Napa Valley, there was the winery, with acres of vineyards to support the enterprise.

"Beside the point," Slater said. He worked for a living, and he worked hard, but he felt no particular need to explain that to this kid or anybody else. "What's your name?"

"Ryder," the boy answered after a moment's hesitation.

"Where do you go to school, Ryder?"

"The same lame place everyone around here goes in the eighth grade. Mustang Creek Middle School."

Slater lifted one hand. "I can do without the attitude," he said.

Ryder recovered quickly. "Sorry," he muttered.

Slater had never been married, but he understood children; he had a daughter, and he'd grown up with two kid brothers, born a year apart and still a riot looking for a place to happen, even in their thirties. He'd broken up more fights than a bouncer at Bad Billie's Biker Bar and Burger Palace on a Saturday night.

"I went to the same school," he said, mostly to keep the conversation going. He was in no hurry for the redhead to call it a night, especially since he didn't know her name yet. "Not a bad deal. Does Mr. Perkins still teach shop?"

Ryder laughed. "Oh yeah. We call him 'The Relic.'"

Slater let the remark pass; it was flippant, but not

mean-spirited. "You couldn't meet a nicer guy, though. Right?"

The kid's expression was suitably sheepish. "True," he admitted.

The stepmother glanced at Slater with some measure of approval, although she still seemed riled.

Slater looked back for the pure pleasure of it. She'd be a whole new experience, this one, and he'd never been afraid of a challenge.

She'd said she was divorced, which begged the question: What damn fool had let *her* get away?

As if she'd guessed what he was thinking—anybody with her looks had to be used to male attention—the redhead narrowed her eyes. Still, Slater thought he saw a glimmer of amusement in them. She'd calmed down considerably, but she wasn't missing a trick.

He grinned slightly. "Cuffs?" he inquired mildly, remembering Ryder's statement a few minutes earlier.

She didn't smile, but that spark was still in her eyes. "That was a reference to my former career," she replied, all business. "I'm an ex-cop." She put out her hand, the motion almost abrupt, and finally introduced herself. "Grace Emery," she said. "These days I run the Bliss River Resort and Spa."

"Ah," Slater said, apropos of nothing in particular. An ex-cop? Hot damn, she could handcuff him anytime. "You must be fairly new around here." If she hadn't been, he would've made her acquaintance before now, or at least heard about her.

Grace nodded. Full of piss-and-vinegar moments before, she looked tired now, and that did something to Slater, although he couldn't have said exactly what that something was. "It's a beautiful place," she said. "Quite a change from Seattle." She stopped, looking uncomfortable, maybe thinking she'd said too much.

Slater wanted to ask about the ex-husband, but the time obviously wasn't right. He waited, sensing that she might say more, despite the misgivings she'd just revealed by clamming up.

Sure enough, she went on. "I'm afraid it's been quite a change for Ryder, too." Another pause. "His dad's military and he's overseas. It's been hard on him— Ryder, I mean."

Slater sympathized. The kid's father was out of the country, he'd moved from a big city in one state to a small town in another, and on top of that, he was fourteen, which was rough in and of itself. When Slater was that age, he'd grown eight inches in a single summer and simultaneously developed a consuming interest in girls without having a clue what to say to them. Oh yeah. He remembered awkward.

He realized Grace's hand was still in his. He let go, albeit reluctantly.

Then, suddenly, he felt as tongue-tied as he ever had at fourteen. "My family's been on this ranch for generations," he heard himself say. "So I can't say I know what it would be like having to start over someplace new." *Shut up, man.* He couldn't seem to follow his own advice. "I travel a lot, and I'm always glad to get back to Mustang Creek."

Grace turned to Ryder, sighed, then looked back at

Slater. "We've taken up enough of your time, Mr. Carson."

Mr. Carson?

"I'll walk you out," he said, still flustered and still trying to shake it off. Ordinarily, he was the proverbial man of few words, but tonight, in the presence of this woman, he was a babbling idiot. "This place is like a maze. I took over my father's office because of the view, but it's clear at the back of the house and—"

Had the woman *asked* for any of this information? No.

What the hell was the matter with him, anyway?

Grace didn't comment. The boy was already on the move, and she simply followed, which shot holes in Slater's theory about their ability to find their way to an exit without his guidance. He gave an internal shrug and trailed behind Grace, enjoying the gentle sway of her hips.

For some reason he wasn't a damn bit tired anymore.

Don't miss ONCE A RANCHER
by Linda Lael Miller.
Available April 2016
wherever HQN books and ebooks are sold.

REQUEST YOUR FREE BOOKS!
2 FREE NOVELS PLUS 2 FREE GIFTS!

HARLEQUIN®

American Romance®

LOVE, HOME & HAPPINESS

YES! Please send me 2 FREE Harlequin® American Romance® novels and my 2 FREE gifts (gifts are worth about $10). After receiving them, if I don't wish to receive any more books, I can return the shipping statement marked "cancel." If I don't cancel, I will receive 4 brand-new novels every month and be billed just $4.74 per book in the U.S. or $5.49 per book in Canada. That's a savings of at least 12% off the cover price! It's quite a bargain! Shipping and handling is just 50¢ per book in the U.S. and 75¢ per book in Canada.* I understand that accepting the 2 free books and gifts places me under no obligation to buy anything. I can always return a shipment and cancel at any time. Even if I never buy another book, the two free books and gifts are mine to keep forever.

154/354 HDN GHZZ

Name _____ (PLEASE PRINT) _____

Address _____ Apt. # _____

City _____ State/Prov. _____ Zip/Postal Code _____

Signature (if under 18, a parent or guardian must sign)

Mail to the **Reader Service:**
IN U.S.A.: P.O. Box 1867, Buffalo, NY 14240-1867
IN CANADA: P.O. Box 609, Fort Erie, Ontario L2A 5X3

Want to try two free books from another line?
Call 1-800-873-8635 or visit www.ReaderService.com.

* Terms and prices subject to change without notice. Prices do not include applicable taxes. Sales tax applicable in N.Y. Canadian residents will be charged applicable taxes. Offer not valid in Quebec. This offer is limited to one order per household. Not valid for current subscribers to Harlequin American Romance books. All orders subject to credit approval. Credit or debit balances in a customer's account(s) may be offset by any other outstanding balance owed by or to the customer. Please allow 4 to 6 weeks for delivery. Offer available while quantities last.

Your Privacy—The Reader Service is committed to protecting your privacy. Our Privacy Policy is available online at www.ReaderService.com or upon request from the Reader Service.

We make a portion of our mailing list available to reputable third parties that offer products we believe may interest you. If you prefer that we not exchange your name with third parties, or if you wish to clarify or modify your communication preferences, please visit us at www.ReaderService.com/consumerschoice or write to us at Reader Service Preference Service, P.O. Box 9062, Buffalo, NY 14240-9062. Include your complete name and address.

"Mrs. Harris?"

Whatever picture of the Ranger Natalie may have had in her mind didn't come close to the sight of the tall, thirtyish, hard-muscled male in a Western shirt, jeans and cowboy boots.

Her gaze flitted over his dark brown hair only to collide with his beautiful hazel eyes appraising her through a dark fringe of lashes.

"I'm Miles Saunders." She felt the stranger's probing look pierce her before he showed her his credentials. That was when she noticed the star on his shirt pocket.

This man is the real thing. The stuff that made the Texas Rangers legendary. She had the strange feeling that she'd seen him somewhere before, but shrugged it off. This was definitely the first time she'd ever met a Ranger.

"Come in." Her voice faltered, mystified by this unexpected visit. She was pretty sure the Rangers didn't investigate a home break-in.

"Thank you." He took a few steps on those long, powerful legs. His presence dominated the kitchen. She invited him to follow her into the living room.

"Please sit down." She indicated the upholstered chair on the other side of the coffee table while she took the matching chair. There was no place else to sit until the destroyed room was put back together.

He did as she asked. "I understand you have a daughter. Is she here?"

The man already knew quite a bit about her, she realized. "No. I left her with my sitter."

He studied one of the framed photos that hadn't been knocked off the end table, even though a drawer had been pulled out. "She looks a lot like you, especially the eyes. She's a little beauty."

Natalie looked quickly at the floor, stunned by the personal comment. He'd sounded sincere. So far everything about him surprised her so much she couldn't think clearly.

He turned to focus his attention on Natalie. "You're very composed for someone who's been through so much."

"I'm trying to hold it together." After all, with her own personal Texas Ranger guarding her and Amy day and night, what was there to be worried about?

Don't miss THE TEXAS RANGER'S FAMILY
by Rebecca Winters, available May 2016 wherever
Harlequin® American Romance®
books and ebooks are sold.

www.Harlequin.com